HACKS

BRIAN KNIGHT

This edition published by Tulpa Books. Copyright © 2018 by Brian Knight. Previously published in 2006 by Delirium Books, 2010 by Darkside Digital, and 2012 by Gallows Press. All rights reserved.

Edited by: Lisa Lee Tone and H Michael Casper.

www.tulpabooks.com

ALSO BY BRIAN KNIGHT

Horror - Novels

- Feral
- Broken Angel
- Hacks

Horror - Chapbooks

- Children of Filth
- Heart of the Monster
- Apocalypse Green
- Johnny Junk
- Death is Blind
- Midnight Blues
- The Beast Inside - The Berserkers, Part 1
- Blood Rage - The Berserkers, Part 2

Horror - Collections

- Dragonfly

The Phoenix Girls - Fantasy

- The Conjuring Glass (Book 1)
- The Crimson Brand (Book 2)
- The Heart of the Phoenix (Book 3)

The Misadventures of Butch Quick - Crime

- A Face Full of Ugly - A Chapbook
- Big Trouble in Little Boots - A Chapbook

For H Casper, who continues to be a good sport.

Blue Mountain Blaze Threatens Anatone.

The blaze spotted early yesterday morning by a Department of Lands employee at the Wenatchee Lookout Tower has now burned thousands of acres of wilderness and forced the evacuation of several high mountain campgrounds.

Fire crews now have the wild fire sixty percent contained to the west and south-west, where it threatened the evacuation of Stentz Springs and Baker's Pond area homes. High winds continue to drive the blaze eastward, where it threatens residents of Anatone.

It is unclear if the fire was started by lightning or humans.

The inmate fire crew from the State Prison in Orofino, Idaho is now working with Washington fire fighters to contain the blaze's eastern front.

A small party rescued by an Air National Guard helicopter crew surveying the area was taken to Sacred Heart Medical Center in Spokane, Washington, and are being questioned.

CHAPTER 1

The Devil's Tail

Aptly named, The Devil's Tail twisted through some of the roughest country the Blue Mountains had to offer. It was a narrow, stony whip crack of a road, thrown into constant darkness by old, leaning fir and pine trees. Ten miles from where The Devil's Tail split from the main forest service road through The Blues, it ended abruptly.

There was no warning, no Twilight-Zone-Sign proclaiming *The End Draweth Nigh* or *Here There Be Monsters*. Just more of the same; a narrow dirt road embedded with stones like small mountains and valleys forged by years of runoff from the spring thaw, the forest's perpetual darkness, and what might be a thousand hidden eyes watching your passage.

And after a last bracing turn of the goat path the forest service called a road, a new world opened up. A vista of open sky, powder blue from horizon to horizon, and the distant green and gray of the mountains on the other side of a deep dark pit that may very well have been a bottomless canyon.

On the flat before the canyon, a half-dozen small cabins stood flanking a larger cabin, three on each side, like old weather-beaten soldiers in line with their commander. The large cabin, a service station fire lookout until the tower two ridges to the west made it obsolete, had been fighting its battle against The Blues for half a century. The smaller cabins had stood beside it a mere thirty years, but were no less eroded by the passage of twenty harsh winters, and eighty seasons of disuse. The forest service turned the old lookout into a lodge, built the smaller cabins around it, and rented them out during the summer.

No one had used them in twenty years.

This mid-July day, comfortably cool in the high mountains, a dozen men were at work undoing twenty years of neglect.

Two men crouched on the roof of the lodge tearing out rotted shingles and replacing them. Another cleared seasons of debris from a large, sunken stone fire ring.

Gasman #1, Galen, stood idle while the hose trailing from the back of his truck pumped propane into an underground tank, while gasman #2, Erick, inspected the copper fuel lines and fittings running to each cabin.

"Is it shut off yet? Drew?" Erick had to shout to be heard over the pumping fuel truck.

A man in forest service green poked his head through an open window a few feet away. "Yeah," he shouted, then nodded for good measure. "That's all of them except those two." He pointed toward the last two cabins to their right.

"Thanks," Erick shouted back. "Let me know when you have the rest shut off."

"Will do, boss," Drew said.

What a fucking week, Drew Williams thought as he pulled his head back into the cabin; unexpected holdups every day, that noisy fucking truck pounding his brain to mush, the forced overtime.

No way in hell the place would be up to snuff by Friday evening. Might as well kiss that goddamn fishing trip he'd planned for this weekend goodbye.

The worst of it was that fucking road. That rutted, rocky bastard would tear his truck apart before this was over, not to mention what it was doing to his back. He hadn't been in this much pain in years, not since the accident had landed him in a hospital bed for a month, and left him pulling light duty for the rest of his working life.

Of course, he was only supervising the work here, but that god damned road was going to kill him.

And all because some rich city cunt decided she had to have this place. How the hell did she even know about it? No one came here anymore.

Drew bent, gasping at the flare of pain in his back, and double checked the gas shutoff valve behind the heater. Closed. Good. Five cabins down, two to go. He wanted nothing more than to lie down on the new bed they'd installed at the insistence of that rich city bitch, pop one of his pills and sleep until it killed the pain. But if he didn't hurry to the next cabin and shut off the gas line ASAP he'd have gasman Erick all over him.

Erick had given Drew hell about having to come out this far on such short notice, and had added a substantial trip charge for his trouble. His disposition had not improved one whit since he'd arrived.

Fucking government contracts, Drew thought. If not for some contract that had probably been negotiated from a comfortable office somewhere in Olympia, he'd have told gasman Erick where to stick it and found someone else to do the job.

"Hurry up," Erick yelled, for what might have been the hundredth time that day. "We have a half-hour to finish this leak check or we'll go into overtime!"

"You poor overworked baby," Drew said, but not loud enough to be heard over the pumping truck. "Wouldn't that be a damned shame."

Drew hurried to the next cabin.

Leak test complete, propane tank filled, Erick shoved a bill into Drew's hand and gave a curt goodbye. Drew gave the propane truck the bird as it vanished around the corner onto The Devil's Tail.

His crew, plus the two carpenters they'd contracted to repair the cabins, were sitting around the stone ring having a break, and a break sounded just fine to Drew. He'd have a piss and a smoke, in that order, then maybe sneak away for a lie down in one of the cabins.

He'd rather have a Percoset and a cold beer to wash it down with.

The lodge's septic tank was full, years of snow runoff and rain had managed to fill it somehow, and the crap man wasn't due for another day. Probably a cracked line from one of the cabins. *Hopefully* just a cracked line. If the tank itself was compromised, there was a whole new set of problems that would probably include the EPA. The toilets in the cabins and lodge were off limits for now, so Drew took the trail through the woods toward the lake, and the only outhouse.

The lake was small and clear. Constant flow from the underground spring that also fed the lodge's well kept it from stagnating. It even had a healthy population of trout. Drew had considered bringing his fishing rod if they did have to work through the weekend, maybe sneak off and throw a line in while the others were working. It wasn't worth his job though, or his retirement. Five years to go now. Just five years and the forest service could take their job and cram it.

Something moved in the trees to his right, and Drew jumped, sending a new lance of pain up his throbbing spine. He scanned the trees before moving on, but saw nothing. Being this far out in the Blues made him nervous as hell. The Devil's Tail belonged to beast, not man, and though it was probably just a startled deer, or maybe a branch-hopping squirrel, mountain lions and bear were too plentiful out here. The bigwigs in Olympia were pushing to reintroduce wolves to the area too. Damned if they weren't bound and determined to kill him before he retired.

When they'd first arrived, this trail had been almost completely swallowed up by the forest. Clearing it so they could take a crap safely had been the first order of business. Other trails led into the woods around the small lake, but he'd steered his men away from those. He did not want anyone going down those trails, specifically the one at the far end of the lake. There were things down there better left unfound.

Let the woods keep them, he thought.

There was another burst of movement in the trees to his right, but Drew ignored it. He unbuckled his belt with one hand while reaching for the outhouse door with the other.

A loud grunt from inside the privy stopped him. The grunt was followed by an explosive, splattering fart.

"Christ, put a muffler on it," he shouted at the outhouse door, then turned back up the trail, the pressure on his bladder growing insistent.

When Drew reached the lodge, the carpenters were back on the roof, but his crew still sat around the stone ring.

Lazy bastards, he thought.

"Drew!"

He turned, and cursed.

"Wadaya, want, Yohan?" He knew what Yohan wanted though. He'd been expecting the man to show up sooner or later.

"Story is someone is renting this dump," Yohan tipped his big John Wayne meets the Great White Hunter hat back and surveyed the area. "Looks like I heard right."

Drew grunted. "How's business?"

"Slow. Who is it, Drew?"

"If I tell you, will you get the hell out of here and let me work?"

"Whatever you say, partner." He tipped Drew an obscene wink. "However you want it."

Drew fished his wallet from his back pocket, withdrew a business card, and handed it over. "That's the lady you want to talk to. She's staying at the Red Lion in Lewiston, but you can reach her on her cell phone."

Yohan smiled, gave Drew a nod. "Thank ya' kindly. It's nice to know some folks still look out for their own."

Their own, Drew thought with disgust.

But he knew Yohan was right. They hadn't been friends in a long damn time, but they did still share one interest, and it was in that interest that Yohan had come. Not just a job, but insurance.

He and Yohan had killed a man once, not far from here, and the evidence of that crime was still out there. Waiting for the wrong person to come nosing around.

Having Yohan on the job was the best insurance against that.

Drew stalked to the far end of the clearing, to the edge of the canyon. His irritation faded as he drew closer to the edge. The view was dizzying, incredible. One of the best The Blues had to offer.

How many hundreds of feet to the bottom?

He had no idea, but the wonder he felt standing over the drop, right at its edge, was laced with a nervous fear.

All it would take was one strong gust, he thought. *Put me right over the edge. I'd die of a heart attack before I came close to hitting bottom.*

Far below where he stood, facing the beautiful abyss, an eagle sailed the wind, letting loose a cry that echoed between the canyon walls.

That, Drew thought as he unzipped, *is not something you see every day.*

He imagined nailing it with a stream of piss as it

passed below, chuckled, and let flow. The stream of urine arched out over the impossible drop like yellow rain.

A crunch of footsteps in dry grass startled him from his happy thoughts, and he turned.

"What the hell's wrong with you? Can't I take a leak without ..."

Drew's next word caught in his throat.

A quick glint of sunlight on steel blinded him. A swishing sound, followed by a wet *rip*.

There was no pain, only a moment of disorientation as the world spun around him, and as Drew fell, he caught a glimpse of his headless body standing on the ledge, dick still in hand. His headless body, and the man standing behind it.

The last thing Drew saw as his head tumbled into that beautiful abyss was his own body leaning forward and following in an ungraceful, flailing swan dive.

CHAPTER 2

The Invitation

Mr. James Eldridge,

I am pleased to invite you to attend this year's Hacks Club, a private retreat for authors and editors whose work I admire. The Hacks meet every year at my invitation for a one week, all expense paid getaway beginning August 20.

I've chosen you as a potential Hack on the strength of your novel, "Burn." I own a copy of the limited edition, leather-bound hardcover, and found it an enjoyable read as well as a great investment.

Most of this year's chosen Hacks are first timers, like yourself. I typically invite only one Hack for a second year, a Veteran Hack to help potential attendees decide if Hacks is worth their time. Veteran Hacks are chosen because I've found them to be the most interesting of the previous year's Hacks. This year's Veteran Hack (I am positive you know him) is back for his third year.

As your host, I will pay all your traveling expenses and arrange for your boarding and food. You will spend a week in seclusion, in the company of some of the finest writers and editors working today.

I ask only three things of you in return. One; bring a pen. I will have copies of your books for you to sign and inscribe. Two; be prepared to share stories and personal experiences, both in and out of the book biz. Three; have a good time. Above all else, I want my Hacks to enjoy their time with each other, and with me, your host.

You'll find contact information in the enclosed card. Please RSVP.

Looking forward to your response,

Susan Bonkowski, collector and fan.

PS. I realize that this is short notice, but one of my Hacks met with ill fortune and is unable to attend. I hope you'll be available to take his place.

The letter arrived by UPS. Jim signed for the envelope, then closed the door against the August heat and took it back to his study, puzzled and a little concerned. The way things were going for him lately, an unexpected return receipt letter could only mean bad news. Usually the UPS man came either with contributor copies of his own books, or contracts. The thin envelope didn't have any books in it, and he wasn't expecting any contracts.

He felt a sudden, cold panic. Maybe it was a contract cancellation, and he was about to become an orphaned author. But no, things were nothing but peachy with his publishers at the moment. He was meeting deadlines, turning in revisions on time, and sales were good. Not mind blowing, but good nonetheless.

He flipped the envelope over and studied the address label. A PO Box in Washington State, a town called Asotin. In lieu of a name, a single word. Hacks.

Jim dropped down into the chair in front of his desk and tore the UPS envelope open. Inside, a smaller envelope, cream colored, with his name printed in calligraphy.

A minute later, when he'd read the letter twice, he shook his head and felt inside the cream envelope, pulling out a small, folded card. Black, with his name in gold. He opened it and found a series of numbers and dots.

What the hell?

Beneath that:

Username: Jim Eldridge.

Password: Hacks6.

Then he understood. The numbers were a server address, the path to a website, but one without a domain name. Whoever this Susan Bonkowski was, she didn't want anyone finding this site by accident, or through a Google search.

"So, I'm a hack now," he said. *A second-string hack at that,* he added silently, then crumpled the letter, envelope, and card into an angry ball before tossing them into the trash can beside his desk.

He didn't have time for this shit. There was work to

do. If he wanted to stay in his editor's good graces, he needed to get busy.

But Jim didn't get his flow back. The damn UPS man had broken his train of thought, and the letter in the waste basket had snagged his interest, against his will. After twenty minutes, mostly spent deleting new lines of dialog that didn't quite ring true, he saved the document and closed Word.

He opened his Internet Explorer, brought up Google, typed up a search for Hacks Club and found a group of kayakers. Their motto, *We Paddle For Pleasure*, made him smile. Might have been an S&M club, if not for the picture of a kayak rocketing over whitewater.

Next in line were a German Goth-Sex website and pages of links to Xbox and PlayStation cheat code sites. He gave up on the third page of Google links, considered for a moment, and surfed to the Horror Writers Association website. He wasn't a member, he'd quit the organization three years back, but he knew a few dozen writers and industry pros who did belong to HWA, and one of his friends, a trustee no less, had loaned Jim his login information to the message board so he could keep track of the book business gossip.

Who did he know who had met with ill fortune lately?

He surfed the message threads for another ten minutes and gave up. The closest he found was an update on Dallas Grant, whose health had been failing for some time now. Nothing recent about that.

What next?

Jim tapped his fingers near his keyboard, resisting the urge to go out for a smoke. He wanted one badly, but he wanted to satisfy his curiosity even more, so he could be done with it and get back to work. He compromised by sliding the window closest to him up and lighting up where he sat. Shelly would throw a shit fit if she caught him, but…

He shoved the thought away. He'd managed to put most of a day behind him without thinking of her. Why ruin a good thing?

If Hacks was an ongoing event, there would surely be something about it somewhere on one of the message boards where procrastinating writers gossiped and goaded each other into flame wars.

He started over with a general search on the Horror Writers Association message board, and found nothing. Next he tried the Shocklines.com board. There were more fans and collectors there than writers, so he didn't expect to find anything there. He didn't. Next, and even more of a long shot, Jim thought, was a charming little place called Message Board of the Damned. Though the normal topic for discussion was horror in print and film, you were just as likely to find anything from political rants, porn spam, to threads dedicated to new and interesting combinations of cuss words.

Jim had never posted there, just lurked and read the threads, but he knew a lot of writers who frequented it.

He did a general search, and to his surprise, found a short thread in the archives from two months back.

Hacks Club Conspiracy, was the header.

The post originator was one Richard Pedroos, known affectionately to the board members as Dickey Pee. He had been banished from the board a few weeks prior for posting the home address of another writer, then threatening to blow his balls off with a shotgun.

Dickey Pee, a self-described Maestro of Dark Fiction, composed the post in his customary style.

I've hearded tails of a socalled Hacks Club, which is the Illuminati of horror fiction and controls are which is published or denied. If anyone hear knows of these Hacks and how I can reach them I would deal with these conspirators, who unfairly blackball me because I am conservative and anti-faggot.

Stop being a bunch of pussys and lets do something about this Hacks conspiracy.

Richard Pedroos.

The board moderator replied first.

Dickey Pee, if you don't cut out the homophobic rants, I will ban you from this board. As for your Hacks conspiracy, never heard of them.

The second response came from a writer Jim knew. He worked as a mechanic by day, and was wildly popular with small press collectors and fans. He hadn't crossed over to the mass market yet, and was always quick to admit he probably never would. They would want him to compromise his style, he said, and he'd give up writing all together before he did that.

Jeff Campbell, known by and referred to simply as *Camp* by his friends and fans, would probably remain a mechanic with that attitude, Jim thought. He respected Camp though, and there was no denying that the man was a phenomenal writer.

Camp had posted:

You're a nut-job, and should be sterilized before you reproduce. Later! Camp.

Jim smiled and scrolled down through a dozen off-topic retorts before he found another relevant post.

I've heard of the Hacks Club, but don't know if any of the stories about them are true. Seems to be more urban legend than fact. I heard that Hacks was started about 30 years ago by Elmore Leonard, and that Stephen King, Peter Straub, Brian Keene, Ira Levin, Richard Laymon, Edward Lee, and F. Paul Wilson have all been members at one time or another.

I've also heard that careers have been made and shattered at meetings of The Hacks Club, but I don't think they are the reason you can't get published, Dickey Pee. You just suck.

The unexpected slamming of the apartment's front door startled Jim. He peeked out the window, saw Shelly's car parked behind the neighbor's at the curb. He checked the clock above his bookshelf and was stunned to see it was a quarter past five in the afternoon. He'd been surfing for almost two hours.

He snuffed his cigarette on the windowsill – his fourth he saw from the dead, crumpled butts lined up on the brick jamb – before sliding the window closed. He'd been chain-smoking without realizing it. He'd barely made it back to his chair before Shelly swept into the room.

In his head, Jim heard the words *hi, honey, I'm home.*

Yeah, right, he thought.

She stood over him, her spiked heels adding another 5 inches to her already impressive six feet. She looked like an Amazon in a miniskirt. Her blond hair was wrapped in a bun too tight to have ridden her head through the hot, humid day. She must have rewrapped it before coming home. The heady, expensive perfume she'd doused herself with before leaving for work that morning now had a hint of Brute cologne mixed with it.

Things like this no longer surprised Jim, but they still pissed him off. She could at least keep up the front and try to hide it until the divorce went through, or she'd managed to find a new place.

She gave a false cough and waved a hand in front of her face. "Are you so fucking lazy you can't lift your ass out of that seat to go outside for your cigarettes?"

Jim's smile felt more like a grimace. "Is that a rhetorical question, or do you expect an answer?"

"Bastard!"

"Bitch!"

Shelly turned on her spike heels and stalked out, slamming his office study behind her.

Fuck it, Jim thought, and reached into the waste basket. He plucked out the balled-up letter, then the card, and smoothed them out on his desk.

* * *

The entrance page to Susan Bonkowski's website was a no

frills affair. White background, no text, no graphics. The page header was blank.

"Shit," Jim said, and slammed his computer mouse on the desktop. All this energy focused on what amounted to a blank webpage.

Then a gray pop-up prompt appeared, asking for a username and password. Jim provided them, glancing at the wrinkled black card for conformation before clicking *Submit*.

An image faded in over the white background, a large cabin, flanked on each side by three smaller cabins. A wall of evergreens stood behind them, and the extreme left, what looked like an abrupt drop into some monumental canyon. Mountains.

The photo was old, grainy, black and white.

A large sign, white letters painted on a large, flat wedge of wood said *The Blue Mountains - The Devil's Tail Lodge*.

Below the picture, *You are invited to this year's meeting of The Hacks Club. Time: August 20-28. Place: The Blue Mountains of Washington State.* Below that, a brief history of The Devil's Tail Lodge.

Jim didn't take the time to read it. On the upper right corner of the webpage was a list of names, and next to each name, icons that read *offline* in red letters, or *online* in green. Jim's name was at the bottom of the list, with a green online icon next to it. The other names, he saw Jeff Campbell's name among them and grinned, were listed as offline, except for the top two.

Jim read the second from the top and laughed out loud. Ryan Stahl, Chief Editor and owner of Delirium Books. Delirium had published Jim's last five novels in limited collector editions before they went to mass market. It was the Delirium edition of *Burn* that Susan Bonkowski had mentioned in his invitation letter.

Susan Bonkowski's name was at the top of the list.

The three of them, collector, editor, and Hack, were all logged in. With as much amusement now as curiosity, Jim clicked the chat button below the names.

CHAPTER 3

Heather Woods

Jim had allowed himself a nap on the first connection, but fought hard to stay awake during the second leg of his eight-hour flight. He meant to see what he could of The Blue Mountains from up high, on his way to the Lewiston, Idaho airport, just across the Idaho/Washington border from Asotin. Not far at all from where his trek to The Devil's Tail was to start. Jim knew from experience if he allowed himself to drift off, he wouldn't wake until touchdown, and he'd miss the view.

To that end he'd gulped cup after cup of strong, bitter airline coffee, and found himself fantasizing about the pretty blonde woman sitting in the opposite row, near the cabin. He wasn't the only one to notice her. After making cruising altitude and giving his obligatory speech over the airplane's loudspeaker, the captain had made a walk-through, and stopped to chat with her. He'd only left her side when a frustrated flight attendant trying to navigate her cart around him, had bumped him hard during her third pass. He'd all but fallen into the blonde's lap, and excused himself back to the cabin, blushing.

Two hours and three trips to the bathroom into the flight, the comfort and quiet of first class overcame him, and he slept. He dreamt absurd dreams of being chased through the woods by an Amazon in high heels and a hockey mask, like Jason wore in Friday The 13th. Instead of a machete, she brandished a copy of their divorce papers.

Touchdown bounced him awake, and he swore, irritated with himself. He'd had a bird's eye view of a mountain range larger than his home state, a panoramic view that gave new meaning to the word wilderness, and he'd missed it.

No worries, he told himself. *I'll have all the mountains I can stand in an hour or two.*

Then, without even realizing it, Jim laughed.

He'd been doing this for the past two weeks, still surprised to find himself headed for what seemed a dream vacation, over two thousand miles from home. A fan had flown him *first class* across the country, so he could sign books, relax, and tell stories.

Just another of life's little surprises.

A happy one this time.

Jim was still grinning as the flight attendant ushered him and the rest of the first-class passengers off the plane to the small airport's single gate.

At an espresso stand a short walk from the baggage claim, Jim had a mocha while he waited for his luggage. Usually a nervous traveler, anxious about missing connections, paranoid about his luggage and afraid of terrorists, this time he was too excited to be nervous.

"Are you Jim Eldridge?"

He'd been busy watching the empty carousel, waiting for his bags, and hadn't noticed the good-looking blonde from first class standing next to him.

Another of life's happy surprises.

His smile stretched wider when he recognized her as the woman the captain had flirted with. Now his view of her was even better. She was diminutive, trim but nicely shaped, with a manner that radiated class.

"Yes." Jim nodded and extended a hand.

She took it in both of hers and gave it a squeeze. Her hands were small. Soft, but strong.

Jim's pulse quickened at her touch. He hoped he wasn't blushing too fiercely.

"I love your work," she said. "Your story *Damned in Paradise* made me cry."

Jim was shocked into silence. *Damned in Paradise* was a short story damned near every short horror market had rejected, and had found life as an afterthought, a filler in a small press collection a few years back.

At last he spoke. "Thanks. I didn't think anyone had actually read that."

"Only your hard-core fans," she said, then winked. "Oops, there's my bag," she said a second later, and started for the luggage carousel.

Jim spotted his two bags, and followed.

"Business or pleasure?" he asked, not wanting to let the conversation go so quickly. Then he cringed, because that sounded so goddamn lame. Being a writer didn't automatically make you a good conversationalist, Jim knew. Boy did he know.

"A little of each," she said, reaching the carousel and waiting for her bag to reach her. "You?"

"Same," he said. "Meeting my editor and a few friends," he added, wanting to sound impressive. Somehow, he didn't want to tell this pretty woman he was here for what amounted to little more than spending a week as some super-fan's pet writer. His bags arrived before hers, and he scooped them up.

"Well, I better run now. My ride is probably waiting outside. Nice meeting you." He set one of his bags down and offered his hand again, but she did not take it.

"Here's my bag. Hold on for a second and I'll walk out with you."

Light traveler, he thought.

"Sure. Anything for a hard-core fan." He cringed again. That was even worse than *business or pleasure*.

She laughed, grabbed a bag, a large yellow duffel that would have looked more at home in a locker room, then took his arm with her other hand and led him away.

As they neared the lobby's exit Jim's heart dropped. A man stood just outside the door in front of a limo, holding a sign that said Eldridge/Woods. Heather Woods, one of his fellow Hacks and the biggest name of the gathering, was probably waiting inside. He was looking forward to meeting her, but was also a bit nervous. He was a fan, and understood from experience what a letdown it usually was meeting your idols.

The woman holding onto his arm, on the other hand, he could spend more time with her.

Farewell, pretty lady, he thought as he pushed the door open. *All good things come to an end.*

The heat came as a bit of a shock after the cool interior of the airport. A fine sweat broke out instantly on his forehead.

Then the fair lady released his arm and pointed at the limo. "Look," she said. "There's our ride."

Jim stopped, rocked forward a bit as she grabbed hold of his arm again and tugged him forward. When she turned to him, a sly smile on her lips, he tried to speak, but all he could manage was a weak cough.

He tried again. "You're Heather Woods?"

Her smile widened, apparently pleased with his discomfort.

"Oh, you've heard of me then?"

Yes, Jim *had* heard of Heather Woods. Who hadn't?

Heather Woods was an honest to God true-life success story in the wonderful, wacky world of publishing. A relative newcomer to the business, she had been published for five years, had only started writing two years prior to that. He'd read that tidbit in an article about her once. Her first novel had sold for the kind of money Jim could only dream about.

Since then she'd become a favorite target of would be and less successful writers. Jealousy, Jim knew, partly because he'd felt some of the same. With only one book, she'd launched the kind of career that coaxed otherwise sane people into the irrational business of fiction writing.

She'd never had anything to do with the large, but rather tight community of genre writers, a diverse and far spread group of people connected by the miracle of the Internet, and Jim thought that was part of it too. She had not paid the same dues they'd been forced to pay; the nose rubbing and schmoozing, reams of rejection letters from bottom-of-the-heap magazines that paid little, if anything at all.

Jim had wondered if their summary dismissal of her was the reason she'd never become more involved with them. Mostly, he supposed, she was just too busy *writing*.

Her novels, campy suspense yarns, he'd heard them called, and sometimes dreck, generally received so-so reviews and were snubbed by the critics, but routinely landed on the New York Times Bestseller list. Dumbfounded by her improbable success, Jim had finally broken down and bought her fourth novel.

He'd finished it in a single afternoon.

It made sense to him then. The critics hated her books because they were pure fun. Other writers, reviewers, and wannabes hated her because she was better than them. Clearly, inarguably better.

That was, in Jim's humble opinion, the simple reason behind her success.

He'd been a fan since then.

Yes, Jim *had* heard of Heather Woods, and he was beyond thrilled to hear that she had, evidently, heard of him too.

Jim talked almost non-stop during the limo ride, but remembered very little of the conversation. He'd switched to fan mode, and as Heather didn't seem to mind, seemed interested in what he had to say in fact, he didn't try to stop himself. At some point she'd turned the conversation to him, and Jim felt himself pulled deftly into a discourse that felt almost like an interview. Personal stuff, but not too personal.

Then, abruptly, the conversion tapered off to silence.

"I'm sorry," she said a minute later, looking out the tinted rear window of the limo. They were crossing a narrow, busy bridge. The Snake River, if he remembered it right. He saw a sign that said Welcome To Washington as they approached the other end.

"About what?" Jim asked.

But she didn't answer. Just stared out the window, slumped back against her side of the seat, head lolling slightly with each bump.

"Heather?"

"I didn't go out today," she said softly. She sounded like a woman talking in her sleep. "I couldn't get out."

Jim shivered a little, reached out and touched her arm. "Heather?"

Her head rolled toward him, facing him, but not seeing him. Her eyes were closed to slits, showing only slivers of white.

"Please," she said. *Pleading.*

"Heather?" Jim gave her a little shake.

Heather jerked awake with a gasp, face pale, eyes wide open. She scanned the inside of the limo, looking like someone lost, then settled with a sigh.

"Are you okay?"

Heather put a hand over her face, rubbed at her eyes. "I am so embarrassed. I'm sorry you had to see that."

The limo took a sharp turn and she fell against him.

"It's okay, Heather. What happened?"

"I just zoned out for a second," she said, straightening in her seat. Her previously shining expression now deadly serious. Jim was sad to see it go. He wished she would smile again.

Heather tapped the tinted glass partition between the driver and them, and it lowered with an electric buzz.

"How much farther to Asotin?"

"Just a few more minutes, ma'am," the driver said, then gave a stiff little nod at the rearview mirror and closed the partition.

Heather rolled down her window, closing her eyes as a warm wind rushed in, throwing her hair around like a blond nimbus. When she turned to him, the smile was back.

"You mind?" She nodded at the open window.

"Not at all," Jim said. "What just happened."

"Oh, that was nothing," she said, in a tone of voice that suggested she had indeed convinced herself of that. "Just needed a little fresh air."

Oh man, Jim thought. *Looks like the duffel isn't the only baggage this pretty lady brought along.*

"This is exciting," Heather said. Her hand crept over the seat between them and gave his a quick squeeze.

"Yes," he said, again hoping he was not blushing too fiercely. "It is."

CHAPTER 4

Earthy Redneck Wit

Everything about Asotin was small. Jim could see from one end of town to the other from where he stood when the driver let him out.

Heather didn't give the man a chance to walk around and open her door, but slid out behind Jim. He watched as she took in the town, her eyes more than bright now. Hungry; taking in *everything* and keeping it. Jim would not be surprised to find this town reincarnated in a future Heather Woods novel.

Townspeople at the quaint little General Store, walking along the street, strolling through the park, watched them, many stopping in their tracks and staring. Jim wondered if they had seen their faces on a dustcover jacket, and he was tempted to cross the street and check the General Store's book rack.

Moments later, the driver removed their luggage from the trunk. He placed all three bags on the ground and slammed the trunk shut, picked them up and led Jim and Heather into the park, toward a small gazebo.

"Good day," he said, giving them a stiff little nod before returning to the limo.

"Hey," Jim said. "You're leaving us *here*?"

The man stopped, turned, gave his stiff nod. "This is where I was told to drop you off." Then, with the hint of a smile, "Don't worry, the others seem to have made it to where you're going."

And he was off.

Barely a minute had passed before a white Jeep pulled up in the park, almost as if it had been parked only a few blocks away, waiting for the limo to leave.

Painted in black, stenciled letters on the doors was *Misery Mountain Guides*, beneath that, a phone number and web address. A man in a large dust-colored Stetson, its brim pinned at the sides and molded to a drooping point up front, poked his head out of the open window.

"Woods and Eldridge?" He called to them. "C'mon, let's go." His voice was slow, with a country twang that sounded affected.

Jim suddenly missed the curt, quiet limo driver.

"What a colorful man," Heather commented as they rose from their uncomfortable gazebo seats. She reached for her bag, but Jim grabbed it first.

"I've got them," Jim said, grunting as he heaved both his bags off the floor with the other hand.

Heather laughed. "Such a gentleman," she said, but pulled her bag from his hand.

The man in the Jeep opened the hatch from the inside, and Jim and Heather loaded them into the back.

Jim closed the hatch, then opened the rear door for Heather.

She rolled her eyes at him. "Were you brought up to be nice to the ladies, or am I just a special case?" she asked.

"A little of both," he said, and climbed in beside her.

"Would you two like a room, or can we get going now?"

"Onward, Jeeves," Heather said, her voice laced with humor.

"No offense, lady," the man said squinting into the rear-view mirror at them, "but you writers are strange."

The man's sullen, almost offended silence, lasted all of a few minutes. By the time they'd left town, climbing a steep, winding grade into the mountains - no towering evergreens here, just rock and a thick cover of dead, wild grass - he'd turned back to them, steering blindly around a sharp curve with one arm, offering the other to them. "Yohan Johnson," he said.

Heather took his outstretched hand, unconcerned. "Heather Woods. Delighted to meet you."

"Jim Eldridge." Jim gave a quick, one-pump shake, hoping that the introductions were over and Yohan would get back to the business of driving.

"So, what's going on up there anyway? Kinda' weird, all you rich and famous folks coming out *here*."

Jim saw Yohan's eyes grow suddenly wide, as if the man were passing an undigested ham hock, suffering a minor heart attack, or had an epiphany.

"You folks're makin' a movie up there, aren't you?" He

drummed his fingers anxiously on the steering wheel. "You are, aren't you?"

"Not as far as I know," Jim said. He didn't bother to tell the man how far from rich and famous he was. Let him at least keep that misconception.

Yohan smiled into the rear-view mirror, then winked.

"I smell ya. Y'all don't need to worry about me blabbin'." He straightened in the front seat, puffed his chest out. "I'll even offer my services. Guide, extra, anything you need."

"Tell you what, if you can keep this under that handsome hat," Heather said, leaning forward and flicking his hat with a finger, pushing it slightly askew. "You do that for us, and I'll see what I can do for you."

"You got it lady," he said, his voice so serious, so solemn, that Jim had to fight back a chuckle.

Heather sat back, head turned to Jim, and leaned in close. For a moment Jim thought she was going to kiss his cheek, and he went tingly and nervous. Instead, she whispered in his ear.

"Let him dream," she said. "Just as long as he doesn't drag half of that little town up here to audition."

"What's that?" Yohan said.

"Just wondering how far out we're going," Jim lied. "Must be pretty far for Mrs. Bonkowski to hire an expert guide."

"Ain't no *expert*," Yohan said. "Nothing but a ten dollar word for a ten cent job."

"Ah, okay," Jim said, only because Yohan was staring at him as if expecting a response of some kind.

"You know what an expert is, doncha?" Yohan's small black eyes stared into the mirror.

"Watch it!" Jim yelled, as the road in front of them seemed to vanish, leaving a windshield full of blue sky.

Yohan gave the road a quick glance and jerked the steering wheel sharply to the left.

"An ex," he explained, "is a has-been, and a spert is something shoots out your dick."

Jim thought he'd heard Yohan wrong until he saw Heather's mouth fall open, eyes wide with surprise. She lifted a hand to her face to cover a blooming smile.

Yohan's eyes were on the road again, one big fist holding the steering wheel, the other shifting down as the incline became even sharper.

"I ain't no dried-up wad," he said. "I'm a professional."

Earthy redneck wit, Jim thought. *Either this guy is as dumb as a horse apple, or I'm just too dense to appreciate his wisdom.*

Hope I don't have to share a cabin with him.

At the top of the grade, an expanse of flat farmland opened before them. The high mountains were still miles away. In the absence of continued conversation, Yohan turned on the radio. Country music flooded the jeep, and Jim groaned.

Next to him, Heather hummed *Let The Sun Shine In.*

Jim stared out the window at the countryside, quaint farmhouses and men on tractors, harvesting wheat, soy, hay, whatever it was they grew up here. Every few minutes he'd look ahead and see the mountains, a little closer each time.

The country music on the radio broke for local news.

Market prices for the various local crops, weather report - *hot, hot, hot!* - and something about a Department of Lands man who'd gone missing. Yohan turned it up a little, frowning.

Heather had given up on *Let The Sun Shine In* and was humming something that sounded suspiciously like *Iron Man*.

The news ended, and Yohan turned the volume down.

"I know that man," he said. The cocky twang, Yohan's affected accent, was gone. He sounded worried. "He was working up around where we're headed when he disappeared."

"Really? I'm sorry to hear that," Heather said.

"You think they'll find him?" Jim asked.

Yohan shrugged.

"Lot of rough country. Lots of places the rescuers won't go. Too much ground to cover." He sighed. "Too many damned mountain lions and bears. Wolves too, now. Been showing up the last year or so, since they reintroduced them back in Montana. Don't know how they're making it all this way, but they are."

Jim supposed that was as good of answer as he would get, so he let it drop.

"Anyway, that's why Mrs. Bonkowski hired me. To keep you all from wandering off." He flashed a self-satisfied grin at them. "Like a celebrity bodyguard."

Jim's stomach lurched as they caught air over a sharp dip, and he saw another small town before them, maybe a tenth the size of the small river town where Yohan had picked them up.

Welcome to Anatone, said an official border sign. Just

past that, a wooden sign, like a miniature billboard - *Population: 45 people - 23 horses - 36 cats - 20 dogs.*

Jim wondered briefly why they hadn't thought to include the cattle he saw grazing in barbwire fenced fields roughly the size of city blocks.

He realized that he was being a bit of an ass, and with a mental apology to the town of Anatone, promised he'd try to keep the attitude squashed. After all, this could be a great time, if he didn't ruin it for himself.

Yohan slowed considerably and turned right halfway through town, onto a road pointing straight at the mountains. A road that quickly turned from paved to single lane gravel, and was quickly swallowed up by the first of the Blue Mountain's evergreens.

Yohan piloted them into the mountains at a speed that Jim would not have dared had he been at the wheel.

Beside Jim, Heather bounced in her seat. He wasn't sure if it was excitement or the combination of the washboard road and worn out shocks. Jim held onto the door handle with one hand, bracing himself against the front passenger seat with the other.

They rocketed past a sign. Jim turned just in time to read it before their swirling dust wiped out the landscape behind them.

Washington Dept. of Lands - Mount Misery.

"Mount Misery?"

"Yup," Yohan said. Then pointed out at his window with a hand Jim would have preferred he kept on the wheel. "Next range over is called Mount Horrible. The first settlers didn't get on too well here."

"It's beautiful," Heather said, her roving eyes taking in as much as the speeding Jeep would allow.

"Gets better," Yohan said. "Wait'll you see the view from the lodge. Hope you brought a camera."

A minute later, Yohan took a sharp, sliding right turn, and darkness swallowed them.

CHAPTER 5

Where the Devil's Tail Ends

No electricity. He should have known that. The cook stoves, heaters, hot water tanks, and lamps were all gas. There was no generator, and his laptop sat dead next to a windup alarm clock that Susan had furnished. It had about eight hours of battery power left, but there was no sense using it up now while he sat, musing, pondering, daydreaming. Trying to come up with a goddamn idea.

So with a yellow legal notepad on his lap and a black gel pen in hand, Bill Koch sat on the flat surface of a boulder, watching the birds fly *below* him. The view both thrilled, and frightened him, and he was glad now that he hadn't insisted on bringing his eight-year-old son, Steven. Bill wouldn't have gotten a moments peace, worrying that Steven might be about to tumble off the edge.

Writer's block. Mental constipation … it sucked, and when he didn't have a channel to pour his never-ending imagination into, it backed up, soured, poisoned him.

He knew from experience he couldn't fight his way through it. The result would be either frustration, which only seemed to solidify the block, or page after page of crap, which was worse.

An abuse of the English language. Unforgivable. Enraging.

Bill had serious anger issues. He knew this. He accepted it and was trying his hardest to overcome them. He suspected it was an impossible battle. Rage was just a part of his makeup.

But sitting here on the rock, in this place, he did not feel the frustration, the approaching anger bubbling up into a full-blown rage. He was calm, and he didn't even need the bottle, which he'd agreed to give up the week of the Hacks retreat.

He was happy.

He wished Camp would hurry up and get his ass here, though. It wouldn't *really* be a party until Camp showed up.

Bill Koch was here, he wrote in deliberate, neat letters, on a sheet from the tablet in his lap, then signed him name below. He tore the sheet out at the perforation, folded it into a paper airplane, and sent it sailing into the canyon below.

A sudden racket near the lodge drew his eyes, and when a cloud of dust cleared, it wasn't Camp's Mustang, but that lunatic guide's white Jeep. The man had grilled Bill halfway here about the movie he thought they were making, not willing to let it go until Bill had finally come unglued.

This is the last time I'm going to say it, there is no fucking movie! Now shut the fuck up and watch the road!

The positive upshot of Bill's tantrum was that Yahoo, as he had come to think of Yohan, *had* shut the fuck up and kept his eyes on the road from then on. With any luck Yahoo would stay out of his airspace from here on out.

Bill turned back to the canyon, searching for his yellow paper airplane, but it was gone now.

A message in a bottle, he thought, *on paper that would rot before it was ever read.* Suddenly he felt very lonely, perched above the wild, green abyss.

Bill shoved the pen in his pocket, stuck the tablet under his arm, and hurried off to welcome the new Hacks.

For a moment Heather thought Jim was going to throttle the yokel behind the wheel.

He seemed to be considering it. He stared at the back of Yohan's head, his mouth a tight thin line. The dust settled and the clearing in front of the lodge slowly came into view. A woman stepped down from the steps of the lodge, waving the dust away from her face.

Susan Bonkowski?

The woman smiled and waved at them, catching Jim's eye. His anger seemed to ebb. The red in his cheeks faded as he took his eyes off Yohan.

"Here we are folks," Yohan said unnecessarily.

Jim waved back to the woman, then said, "You okay, Heather?"

"Sure I am," she said, her heart fluttering in her chest, her hands clutching her knees to keep them from shaking.

Exhilaration was one thing, she liked a healthy shot of adrenaline as much as the next person, but when Yohan careened onto that last narrow road, he had crossed the line to reckless. She wondered if he was trying to scare them, or if he was just that stupid.

"Hope I didn't shake you up too much. Maybe you creative types aren't as sturdy as you think." He grinned. A hard, humorless grin. His head turned toward the approaching woman, and he lowered his voice a little. "You're lucky I'll be around to handle any rough stuff, should it come to that."

Heather sighed. She had no comeback, no good-natured retort. All that was lost when the Jeep went into a fishtailing spinout around that last bend.

Jim looked like he was about to say something, but Heather never found out what it was. Their doors creaked open in tandem, letting in the comfortably cool mountain air.

The man who had opened her door was handsome, bald, with a few days' worth of stubble covering his cheeks and chin. He had tired eyes, which he turned on the driver's seat. He whispered something that might have been *douchebag,* and helped her out.

The woman who'd opened Jim's door, their hostess Heather assumed, seemed to be avoiding looking at Yohan. Her smile looked forced.

She took Jim's hand and helped him out of the Jeep.

"I'm very pleased to meet you both," she said. Her eyes moved from Jim to Heather. "I'm Susan Bonkowski. Welcome to Hacks."

Jim checked his temper for Heather and Susan's sake, but it took all the self-control he possessed not to pull that freak in the cowboy hat out through his window and do something antisocial to him.

Smug little shit-kicker!

"Pleased to meet you," Jim said, giving Susan's hand a light squeeze. "Appreciate the invitation."

Bill Koch, Jim recognized him from dust jacket pictures, helped Heather from her side of the Jeep. Jim saw her hand shaking in his.

Bill stood calm, eyes locked on the Jeep's driver's. Steady, unblinking eyes. Sniper's eyes.

The trunk door popped open, and Jim hurried to get the luggage. Bill walked Heather toward the lodge, introducing himself as Jim hefted their bags and slammed the trunk. This time she didn't object to his carrying her luggage. A few seconds later Heather stepped inside, and Bill joined him by the Jeep.

Susan, leaning in through the driver's window, had quiet words with Yohan.

"Hand one of those over, man," Bill said. He took Heather's bag in his left hand and extended his right.

Smiling, Jim shook it.

"Jim Eldridge, right?"

"Yeah. Bill Koch?"

"Guilty," Bill said, and after giving the Jeep a last, scorching look, led Jim to the lodge.

"If she doesn't fire Yahoo I'm gonna end up kicking his ass."

Yahoo. Jim liked that.

"Don't think he likes us much."

Bill answered with a commiserating grunt. "He's lucky Camp is driving himself."

Jim had heard stories about Camp; his antics and temper, and he thought Bill had a fair point. If someone decided to hand Yohan, or Yahoo, as Bill had dubbed him, his ass, it would be Camp. Not just another loud, anonymous Internet mouth, Camp had never had a problem mixing it up in real life. Camp had been at the center of a near riot at a hotel hosting the World Horror Convention only a few years ago. Bill had been there with him, raising holy hell, but he seemed to have calmed down a little since then.

Camp had taken up his slack.

"Who's all here so far," Jim asked.

"Me, thee, the lovely lady you rode in with ..." He paused for moment, then asked, "is that Heather Woods?"

"Yeah."

Bill nodded. "Younger than I expected. Prettier too. Wonder why they're using a fake picture in her bio."

That's when it hit Jim, stopping him in his tracks as they crossed the deck to the lodge. The picture on the back cover of her books was not the woman waiting inside for them. The woman on the back cover of her books was older, with hair somewhere between blond and silver. Her face was thinner, not wrinkled, but sour looking.

That's why I didn't recognize her.

"Ryan Stahl is around somewhere. He rode up with Susan."

They crossed the threshold into the lodge. Jim was relieved to see the place was not as primitive as he'd imagined. It looked like an army of maids had been through recently, rubbing out every speck of dust that had settled over the years. The walls looked freshly painted, the hard wood floors scrubbed and waxed, even the high cathedral ceiling was clean.

Several gas lamps in brass sconces were mounted to the walls and an old wagon wheel chandelier hung from the ceiling by a tarnished chain. Twelve glass globes circled the outer edge of the wheel, and Jim tracked the suspending chain along the ceiling's central beam to the wall near the fireplace, where it hung almost to the floor, one of the links held by a large hook on the wall.

Oil lamps, probably. He wondered if they still worked.

Heather sat on a sofa in the center of the room, examining stacks of books on a coffee table in front of her. Looking settled again.

Most of the books were hardcovers, many of those were limited editions. A stack of mass market paperbacks sat alone on the fringe, one of Heather's on top.

Jim and Bill set the bags next to the hearth and went to join her.

"Oh, this is gorgeous!" Heather's hands hovered over a leather-bound volume, as if they wanted badly to touch it, but didn't quite dare.

One of Jeff Campbell's, Jim noticed. He leaned over the table for a closer look.

Bill laughed. "Camp is going to shit when he sees that. That book goes for around five hundred on eBay these days. He sold his copies to buy one of those Semerling's that Repairman Jack uses and has regretted it ever since."

"Who's Repairman Jack?" Heather asked.

Bill looked horrified. "Good lord! Did you hear that, Jim?"

"I did," Jim said, shaking his head. He felt better now too, maybe it was the vision of Heather looking prettier than ever, sitting there with that look of absolute awe, her lips curved into that enchanting smile again.

They sat on either side of her, Jim picking up one of her paperbacks, an advance copy of a novel that hadn't even been released yet, Bill throwing an arm casually over her shoulder. She smiled at them in turn, looking embarrassed, but pleased to be the center of their attention.

"We're going to have to fix that," Bill said. "I've read your work, and trust me, Repairman Jack will be right up your alley."

Jim smiled. He'd had second thoughts about agreeing to come to this Hacks thing, but they were gone now. Meeting Heather had been a wonderful start to what promised to be an excellent vacation.

And when it ended, a thought Jim decided to put out of his mind, Shelly would be gone, the rest of their short, childless mistake of a marriage put to death by their lawyers. With any luck, she wouldn't take him for every penny he'd ever made or would make.

Life, for the moment, was good.

CHAPTER 6
The Editor

The Devil's Tail Ridge. An island surrounded by a sea of air. Wooded slopes to the east and west, some areas gradual enough to climb, others dangerously steep. To the north was the great, straight drop into the canyon. To the south, the main road out of the Blues.

Ryan Stahl didn't know these trails, but he wasn't too worried. Although the woods were strange to him, the layout was easy. Even if he got lost, as long as the sun was out, he wouldn't stay lost. Walking south would lead him in the right direction.

Circling the small lake, he got a good look into the surprisingly clear water. There was enough fish to make him excited for the next morning, when he would rise before the sun and maybe catch his breakfast while the others slept.

He saw a cluster of Huckleberry bushes full of plump purple berries, and stooped to examine them. He plucked a few and popped them into his mouth.

"Oh, yeah," he said before rising and continuing down the trail.

Really, when it comes down to it, woods are woods. Mountains are mountains. Ryan knew what he was doing. If he closed his eyes and breathed in the pine and fir and moss, tasted the berries in his mouth, it was just like being home again.

Ryan lived in the suburbs now, but he'd been raised in the boondocks. The mountains and woods were dear to him, his favorite places to be. He was having the time of his life.

Doing Susan a hell of a favor too.

On the far side of the lake now, he stopped to rest, sitting on the stony edge of the trail, facing the lake, watching the ripples of feeding trout. Behind him, a narrow strip of woods, and then a steep decline to the canyon.

Something rustled in the trees behind him, so faint only someone deeply in tune with the sounds of the forest would even notice it. He turned, startled, and saw the outline of a figure darting away through the trees. Filtering light caught the figure, throwing shadow from the trees over it like a veil. It looked huge, hulking. If not for the way it ran, Ryan would have thought it was a bear, but he knew better. It was a man, running through the trees.

"Hey!" Ryan stood, put a shading hand over his eyes. Low branches swayed where the man had passed. In his sudden absence, silence. No singing birds. No chirping bugs. Nothing scurrying through the high limbs.

Probably that asshole Yohan sneaking around in the twigs, trying to spook him. Having a laugh at his expense.

Creepy bastard.

"You are one weird mother-fucker," he said, loud enough for someone crouching nearby to hear, but not loud enough to carry across the lake.

Ryan moved along, suddenly wishing he had brought a gun.

Just Yohan, he was sure of it, but the creepy bastard *had* spooked him a little.

Spooked or not, he had ground to cover. Once he'd circled the lake, he'd trek deeper into the woods. If Susan was reasonably sure that he'd learned the immediate area, she'd be able to fire Yohan, and that was just fine with Ryan. Yohan was the kind of back woods dimwit that gave all country people a bad name.

Ryan's mom had called it *Small Town, Small Mind Syndrome*, and he used to hate that, but she was right.

He'd left his hometown five years ago for work in Flint, Michigan, but he went home every year, twice a year when he could afford it, to camp in the mountains near his old home. Every year he passed through the small town he'd grown up in, and every time he got the Outsider Stare, even from people who remembered him. And his old friends, if they did stop to talk with him, were patronizing, even hostile.

He'd sensed that hostility, that country boy superiority, in Yohan, and hated the smug bastard for it.

He wondered what the others would make of Yohan, and cringed. Camp and Koch wouldn't take his shit, they'd shut him down quick and have a good laugh about it later. Jim had a temper too, but he would bottle up every little frustration and annoyance until his cork popped and he exploded. That worried Ryan. He liked Jim, but he also liked Susan, and was hoping she would invite him to next year's Hacks Club. Beyond being a good time, Ryan was growing very fond of Susan.

Rich was a good man, but he was gone. Susan was alone now.

Too soon, he reminded himself. *Just be her friend, be the best Hack you can be, and get invited back next year.*

Next year. Yes. It was still too soon now, but maybe next year...

Ryan saw this year's Hacks retreat going one of two ways: either Susan would fire Yohan, and he would take on the additional, but not unpleasant task of trail guide, or the jackass would get on everyone's nerves so badly he'd get an ass kicking. If he stayed on, Ryan was sure Yohan would spoil everyone's time, Susan's most of all.

Either way, Ryan was sure that Yohan, or different variations of him, would die horrible and painful deaths in at least a half-dozen novels in the next few years.

Ryan would probably publish one or two of them himself.

Not that Yohan would ever notice. As he'd told Ryan on more than one occasion since meeting, *I don't like all that made up shit, least not to read. If I want a story I'll turn on the boob tube.*

Susan was nervous about doing this on her own, Ryan's constant reassurance, and his promise to help with the planning if and when she needed help, was one of the reasons she'd gone through with it this year, rather than letting the Hacks Club die out and fade away. She enjoyed the retreats as much as Rich had. Books were in her blood.

It was an affliction Ryan himself shared.

He'd been an avid reader from early childhood, an aspiring writer since his teens, and had even published some short stories in small press magazines. He didn't discover his true passion until later though, while editing an anthology. The original publisher went out of business before the book came out, so Ryan had decided to publish it himself.

Delirium Books was born, and within five years was doing well enough for him to quit his day job. He was now a full-time publisher.

Humming, he finished his circuit around the lake, then started for the closest trail leading into the trees. There were close to a dozen of them just on this side of the ridge. He imagined some of them were overgrown, maybe impassable. He didn't want to lead a bunch of city slicker Hacks down one of the bad trails and get them all scratched up.

He entered the shadowy darkness of the first trail, ears tuned for cracking twigs or rustling brush, the sound of another man flanking him, following him as he left familiar territory behind.

Ryan heard nothing, but couldn't shake the sense that unseen eyes watched him, marked him.

After having words with Yohan, Susan had sneaked away to the nearest empty cabin, shut and locked the door, then laid down on the crisp white linen of the small bed and cried.

She hadn't wanted to have that talk, but Yohan forced her into it. She was almost certain Heather and Jim would demand rides back to the airport. Heather especially looked shaken getting out of that bastard's Jeep. Yohan didn't like them, Susan could tell, and he was getting bolder with his animosity, trying to intimidate people.

He was upsetting her Hacks, thereby upsetting her. Worse than that, she was frightened of him, and she was furious with herself for letting him get to her. He had scared her, and he knew it. That was the worst of it.

She wished Rich was still with her. Rich was strong, a man with presence. Yohan would have not have been so bold if he was here.

Or Ryan. Ryan wasn't afraid of Yohan, and she thought he understood the strange guide better than she did. He wasn't some *city-raised tenderfoot.*

Lady, if I have to spend the week babysitting a bunch of city-raised tenderfoots, Yohan had said, *I am damn sure going to get a premium for my time. And I'll tell you something else, I'm not going to take any shit from them. I know their kind, and they ain't half as smart as they think.*

Ryan had grown up in country like this, around people like Yohan.

She wouldn't have hired him at all if not for that lost Department of Lands employee, she felt a pang of guilt and began to sob harder.

She damn sure didn't want to lose any of her Hacks.

I have to go to the lodge, she thought. *I have to get myself under control. They're going to wonder where I am.*

She lay, face buried in a pillow, until she'd gotten control of herself. Then she rose, wiping tears from her eyes as she walked to the door. On her way out she said, "Please, Ryan, learn those trails."

Then she could get rid of Yohan. She'd fire that bastard in a minute, and Ryan could take his place.

I don't have the guts to do it, she thought, *I'll have Ryan do it.*

Susan managed a smile. Ryan might enjoy that particular chore. If he could get rid of Yohan for her, Ryan was a shoo-in for Veteran Hack again next year.

That is, if she didn't ruin it, if she didn't screw it up so badly that he wouldn't want to come back at all.

Susan started back to the main lodge. A cool mountain breeze played through her hair.

Somewhere in the woods, somebody screamed.

Heather picked up the book she'd been ogling, fingers brushing the soft black leather binding. When the shrill scream echoed across the valley, she let out a small, startled cry of her own, and pulled her hand back as if the book had tried to bite it.

"What in the hell was that?" Jim said.

Bill didn't respond. He sat up, and then bolted for the front door.

Jim and Heather followed.

They found Susan standing outside, frozen in mid-stride, turned and staring in the direction of the woods.

"What's up?" Bill asked.

"Ryan's out there," was all Susan managed before Bill's quick stride became a sprint.

Jim started to follow, but Susan grabbed his arm.

"He went down that trail," she pointed past the furthest of the smaller cabins, "down to the lake."

Jim nodded and hurried after Bill.

At the mouth of the trail, Bill waited for him to catch up.

"Down by the lake," Jim managed between gasps for air. "He's checking out the trails."

Bill nodded. "Let's move."

Jim chased him down the trail, sliding in the dirt, nearly tripping over the exposed corner of a small boulder, working hard just to keep Bill in sight.

Bill handled the rough trail as if he were jogging through a city park.

At last the small lake came into view, and Bill stopped. Jim caught him at a fork in the trail, winded, hunched over, hands on his knees and trying not to collapse. Bill, barely breathing, poised like a predator smelling prey. They could see the trail circling the lake, the left fork clear of branching trails, nothing but a thin strip of trees and what looked like a drop into the canyon behind them. The right fork passed a handful of overgrown trails.

Bill moved again, grabbing Jim's arm and dragging him along. "Take that one," he said, pointing at the first. "I'll take the next. Watch for sign, turn back if you don't find anything after five minutes."

"Sign?"

"Footprints, broken limbs, blood. Anything."

Blood.

Jim felt suddenly cold, small. He gulped. "You think something got him in there?"

"Beats me," Bill said. He shoved Jim into the mouth of the first trail, and then moved toward the second.

Jim hesitated, told himself to quit being a wimp, then moved quickly into the evergreen darkness. He watched the ground as he moved, and saw what might have been a boot's scuff marks in the dirt and carpet of pine needles. After a few minutes, it was hard to be certain when you were concentrating on the terrain, he'd found nothing else. No broken limbs, shirt scraps, or signs of struggle. No blood. Thank God for that.

He was still moving, eyes scanning the carpet of needles, when he nearly ran into Bill.

"Whoa, slick."

Jim jerked his head upward, sliding to a stop, shocked to see Bill standing before him.

"It loops around," Bill said, turning back and running the way he'd come. "Thought it might have when I saw tracks leading toward the lake."

Jim followed. "I found a few footprints, but that's it."

They emerged a few minutes later by the lake, and moved to the next set of trails down the line.

Jim took the first, and was barely ten yards in before he met a dead end of fallen trees and brush.

Back to the lake, he passed the next path, Bill had taken it, and turned onto another. He found nothing, not even the odd scuffing of the thick carpet of needles.

How long had he been running down this trail?

He wished he'd brought a watch with him.

This trail ran straight through the woods, had not turned at all as far as he could tell. No end in sight, and no sign of Ryan.

"Fuck!"

Jim stopped, debated, then turned back toward the lake.

When he emerged, there was a skinny man with shoulder length black hair under a well-worn green

New York Jets cap waiting for him. He held a very large gun.

"Yo! Ryan?"

Jim took a second to catch his breath. "Jim ... Eldridge."

The man nodded and lowered the gun, then looked past him, a hint of a smile brightening his grim face. "Bill!"

Jim turned and saw Bill emerge from the mouth of a trail some fifty feet from them.

Bill nodded. "Hey, Camp. You guys find him yet?"

Jim shook his head and started toward him. Behind him, Camp said, "Nada."

And then they did.

Ryan staggered from the mouth of the last trail at the far end of the lake, holding a cupped palm to his forehead. Blood streamed from behind his hand, streaking his cheek.

"No need for the search party," Ryan said, an embarrassed grin on his face, "but thanks anyway."

He knelt on the stone strewn shore of the lake, cupping water with his hands, washing the blood from his face.

Jim, removed his tee-shirt, wetted it, handed it to Ryan to clean the cut on his head.

"Dude, you're blinding me," Bill said, squinting and averting his gaze. "Get some sun on those tits."

Ryan let out a surprised bark of laughter.

Still winded from the unaccustomed workout, Jim's laughter quickly dissolved into coughing.

So this is why I quit smoking.

"What happened?" he said when he was capable of speaking again.

Camp, standing on the trail above them, the gun still in his hand, turned.

"Bear," Ryan said. "Scared the crap out of me." He rose and pressed Jim's tee-shirt to the cut on his head. "Don't worry, it's already dead."

Camp, who had leveled his gun at the mouth of the trail when Ryan said bear, relaxed and lowered it again.

Jim, Ryan, and Bill joined him on the lake trail.

"I know there are bear around here, but they usually make themselves scarce when people are around. I was making a lot of noise going through, so I didn't expect it." Ryan shrugged, pulled the makeshift bandage from his head, and frowned at the fresh blood. "I turned a corner, found the damn thing rearing up at me, and fell down trying to run. Cut my head when I fell."

"How does a dead bear rear up?" Bill asked.

"Because someone strung it up between the trees."

"Poachers," Camp said.

"That's my guess," Ryan said. "Whoever it was, they cut its head off for a trophy."

"Why the hell would they string it up?" Jim wondered aloud.

Ryan shook his head. "Sick joke maybe. Figured they'd scare the crap out of the next hiker that came along. It's been there a while," he added. "I thought the smell was a dead fox or deer at first."

Camp tried, and failed, to hide a grin behind his free hand. "Worked, didn't it?"

"Fucking-a it did," Ryan said. "Guys, let's not tell the

ladies about it, okay? No need to scare them. Whoever did it is probably long gone by now."

"If they're not," Camp said, but he didn't elaborate.

He thumbed the safety switch and slipped his gun into a holster strapped to his lower back, concealed under his baggy shirt. Jim knew, from his limited research on the subject of firearms, that it was called a C.Y.A. holster – Conceal Your Auto, sometimes jokingly referred to as Cover Your Ass.

He was almost certain Camp didn't have a license to carry in Washington State, let alone carry concealed, but decided not to make an issue of it. He felt a little safer out there knowing one of them was armed.

Ryan examined the bloody shirt again. "Sorry, Jim. I owe you a new shirt."

"Don't worry about it," Jim said. "Let's get the hell out of here."

Grinning, Bill said, "Fuck that, I wanna see that motherfucker. How 'bout you, Camp?"

"I don't *want* to see it." Camp smiled. "I've *got* to see it."

"Susan's scared half to death," Jim said, turning his eyes back toward the path to the lodge.

Ryan looked torn between satisfying Bill and Camp's curiosity, and getting back to the lodge.

"C'mon." Bill nudged Ryan. "You know you want to show us."

"Ah, what the hell." Then to Jim, "We'll be quick."

"Sweet," Camp said, and led the way down the trail.

Ryan and Bill followed him in.

Jim shrugged, and followed.

The trail was long, winding, descending into a valley Jim knew would eventually lead them to the canyon below if they followed it long enough. The Department of Lands hadn't groomed this one as they had a few other others. Brush and limbs choked the trail, making it narrower by the step it seemed.

Stones jutted from the beaten dirt, and exposed tree roots snatched at their feet.

"You must have screamed like a banshee for us to hear you all the way at the cabins," Bill mused aloud, smiling at Ryan.

Ryan affected deafness, but grimaced.

"How much further?" Camp turned back to Ryan, also grinning.

"Just around here," Ryan said, as they approached another bend in the trail.

Camp was the first around the bend. He stopped, hands on hips. "Fuck me! Look at that big son-of-a-bitch!"

Bill stopped next to Camp and tilted his head up. Had to tilt his head up to take in the entirety of the decapitated monster that blocked their path.

"Doesn't look too old," he said.

"Smells old," Jim said, stepping up behind them for his look. "Jesus Christ, that's a big bastard!"

"Yes," Ryan agreed silently. It was one of the biggest he'd ever seen, dead or alive.

The monster stood in a giant X before them, its shaggy, matted pelt obscured by a loose cloud of flies. Heavy ropes bound its arm and legs to nearby trees, keeping it upright. The trees bowed under their burden. Congealed blood stained the bear's stumped neck and massive chest. A hint of raw meat could be seen through the thicker cloud of flies swarming where a head used to be.

No maggots squirming around the exposed flesh, but there would be soon.

The corpse wasn't as old as Ryan had let on, but they didn't question him. He would not say different to them now. If they questioned him about it, he would tell them what he really thought, but for now he'd let the lie stand.

He had his reasons.

Next to him, Jim began to cough, a cough that sounded a lot like gagging.

"We better get back, guys. Before Susan sends Yohan after us."

Jim nodded, looking grateful to be moving away from the source of the wild, rancid smell.

Bill scowled.

"Let her send him." He cracked his knuckles. "We could string him up with Harry The Headless Bear. They could keep each other company."

CHAPTER 7

Hacks

None of them talked about what had gone down in the woods, only that Ryan had been startled by a deer, and he'd fallen. Ryan flushed while they told their false story.

Susan's spirits improved at that news. Sure, she'd been scared, but it had turned out to be nothing, had in fact been a bit of an adventure. The four of them assured her there was nothing much interesting beyond the lake, nothing she'd need a guide for, and that pleased her even more.

The rest of the Hacks arrived over the next few hours, and all seemed in good enough shape, despite the fact that a sullen Yohan had dropped them off. It looked like Susan's talk had worked, at least for the time being.

Tracy West and Michael Smith, Jim had always thought that Michael Smith was a pen name, but it turned out not to be, arrived first. Tracy seemed in awe of their surroundings. Michael bounded from Yohan's Jeep like a sugared-up kid, and made a bouncing, jogging circuit of the clearing, stopping only once to stand with his hands on his hips and stare down into the canyon.

Susan welcomed them in front of the main lodge while the others watched through the windows. With nearly the full party present, the lodge had taken on the feeling of a hotel lobby at the beginning of a convention, except smaller, cozier. Jim had donned a new shirt, a Hawaiian style short sleeve shirt, flashy and bright with hibiscus blossoms and other exotic flowers. Ryan sported a proper bandage where he'd cut his head, but seemed none the worse for wear.

H Casper was the last to arrive. He yawned, and gave the area an apathetic glance, looked annoyed as he hoisted his bulk from the back of the Jeep, supremely bored as he strode toward the lodge. A light breeze blew fine wisps of gray hair around his head like smoke.

"Someone call security," Camp said. "That guy is a wild man."

Jim wasn't sure whether to laugh or not, so he settled into a polite smile.

"Shit," Bill said. "I thought he'd blow us off for sure."

Ryan stood behind them, watching Casper's slow progress. "He always looks pissed, but he's all right. He was at my first Hacks retreat."

Camp and Bill turned to him in unison, eyebrows raised in twin expressions of interest.

"I asked him to be the guest of honor at the last Horrorfind Convention," Bill said. "He turned me down."

Bill's hand was in almost every horror convention Jim had heard of in the past five years, sometimes as an organizer, sometimes as security.

Heather, Tracy, and Michael sat on the sofa in the middle of the room, examining the collected books Susan had brought for them to sign. Heather had, with Susan's permission, finally worked up the courage to open Camp's fancy leather bound book.

Camp had all but drooled when he saw it among the stacks.

Camp kept his voice low as he spoke his next words, evidently not wanting the others at the table to hear. He didn't seem to mind Jim hearing, the four of them already shared one secret, so what was another. "I've heard old H Casper is a real bastard."

"Naw," Ryan said. "He's very private, but once you get to know him, he's a good guy."

"I've always wondered what the H stood for," Jim said.

"Doesn't stand for anything," Ryan said. He smiled at Jim's puzzled look. "H isn't an initial. It's his name."

At last Casper mounted the porch, stopping for a moment to glance through at Jim, Bill, Camp, and Ryan, then nodding before stepping through the door Susan held open for him.

"Thank you, Susan." His soft, easy voice didn't match his gruff face. He gripped her wrist and gave it a gentle shake. "I was so sorry to hear about Richard. I enjoyed his company very much."

It was like a cloud falling over her face, Jim noted, for just a moment her expression darkened, but she recovered quickly and gave Casper a little smile.

"Thank you," she said. "I know Rich enjoyed your company too."

Jim saw Heather rise and gaze at Casper as she had

upon the arrival of all the others, looking more like a nervous fan than a contemporary. Jim wondered if she had never met another writer, and the more he thought about it, the more likely it seemed. She seemed to recognize them all by sight, but none of them, including Jim, had recognized her.

Jim glanced out the window and saw Yohan sitting in his Jeep, glaring at them openly. Fighting an overwhelming urge to close the window shutters, he joined the crowd gathering around Susan and Casper.

After a final round of introductions that brought to mind the goodnight scene in *The Waltons*, Susan said, "Now that we're all here, let's have a seat and begin."

This was more exciting than Heather had imagined. She'd read everyone in attendance, and had always enjoyed their work. She was nervous though. She knew from eavesdropping on some of the Internet message boards that writers frequented that she was a bit of a joke in the business. Jim and Bill had admitted to reading and liking her books, and that did make her feel better.

She sat at the left end of the sofa, Jim at her right, and Casper in a large, overstuffed chair at her left.

H Casper was an old favorite of hers. She'd loved his work when she was a shy teen, hiding from the reality of high-school cliques and hormonal boys. H Casper's odd but wonderful words had been her escape whenever she needed it, and the reason she'd wanted to be a writer since she could remember.

Meeting him was also a bit of a letdown though. His face, eternally young in the dust jacket photos with his mischievous grin and dark hair, now seemed sour, and far too tired. She knew she should have been prepared for that, but it didn't make it any easier.

In every other way though, he was a delight.

Casper was also a legend.

Growing up in England had left him with a trace of an accent. His every gesture seemed refined, and he had greeted them, giving each a few words in turn, shaking the men's hands briskly. He had taken Tracy's and her wrists in that same two-handed pump he'd greeted Susan with. A gesture at once intimate and comforting.

The others were great too.

Bill and Jeff, Camp to his friends, promised to be very interesting. Bill seemed intense and impulsive, and Camp a bit of a wild man. They seemed to know each other well, and she could imagine them cutting up whenever they got together. The lives of the party.

Michael was like a whirlwind in a black shirt and blue jeans, barely contained. Even sitting in a folding chair at the other end of the couch, he was in constant motion, feet tapping, fingers drumming on his knees, eyes twitching manically around the room. Heather wondered, a little uneasily, if he was a coke-head. She'd had experience with coke-heads and he seemed to fit that bill. She chased the unkind thought away.

Ryan seemed the steadiest of the bunch, almost sedate. He'd asked if they could speak in private later, when they had a chance. Heather was quite curious as to what it might be about.

Tracy was outgoing, maybe a little over friendly with the men. She seemed to hang off them in turn, dominating the conversation by force of distraction. She came off a little ditzy, but Heather knew she was not, and suspected that Tracy was sizing the guys up, one at a time, getting a feel for the selection. She wondered how many times Tracy would get laid by the end of the week.

More power to her, Heather thought, but not without a touch of jealousy as she thought of Jim sitting next to her.

She hadn't worked out how she felt about Jim yet, but she thought that her interest might be more than casual. It had been years, too many of them, since she'd taken more than a passing interest in any man.

Her last had left her with a bad taste for them.

Heather hadn't yet gotten a feel for Susan, and in that regard this whole thing was still a bit of a mystery. But as Susan stood before them, getting ready for what felt like an official speech, Heather knew her questions about the hostess, and the gathering, would soon be answered.

For now, she was happy to sit back and enjoy the mystery.

For a moment, Susan could not find her voice. She stood in front of her guests, temporarily frozen while they waited, showing a range of emotions from mild interest to hand wringing anxiety.

It should be Rich up here. This is the part he was so good at.

She took a deep breath and found her voice.

"I'm pleased to welcome you to the ninth annual meeting of The Hacks Club. You're all here because you've singled yourselves out as being amongst the best writers," she nodded to Ryan, "and editors, working in speculative fiction today."

Smiles, a few muttered thank yous, and some blushing answered her kind words.

Michael was tapping out an energetic drum line on his knees.

Bill and Camp nudged each other, grinning like lunatics.

Casper's eyes drooped, as if he was about to drift off at any moment, but he did manage a smile.

Jim watched her, but most of his attention seemed very much focused on Heather, who had put an arm over his shoulder, her face glowing with excitement.

Tracy's eyes kept stealing shrewd glances at the others.

Ryan smiled encouragingly, but seemed otherwise unimpressed. This, Susan knew, was old hat for him.

Susan motioned toward the fireplace, and the others turned toward it. Eight large photographs lined the mantel in identical silver frames with the word Hacks engraved upon them. "As you can see, you're in good company."

In each photograph was a previous years Hacks Club. All the old Hacks smiled down at them, and she saw looks of recognition on several of her new Hacks' faces. Mixed among the small press and mid-list faces were several top names. Casper was clearly visible on one of them, and Ryan in two.

"My late husband started the Hacks club nine years ago as a way of encouraging his favorite lesser known writers, and to thank the more successful for their contributions to a genre he loved."

Susan felt pressure behind her chest, and the heat of fresh tears trying to escape her eyes. This happened whenever she thought about Rich. She braced herself against them, and continued.

"My husband passed away late last year, but left his lifelong love of stories, and the writers who tell them, with me. I could not let Hacks die with Rich. It would have been like watching him die all over again. So, with the encouragement and help of a dear friend," she glanced at Ryan, who smiled again and nodded a silent *you're welcome*, "I've brought you all together for what I hope will be the best Hacks yet."

Susan sighed, steadied herself, and concluded.

"I'd like to dedicate this year's Hacks Club to the memory of my late husband, Richard Bonkowski. Most of you never knew him, but he knew you. Your words brought him pleasure to the last day of his life."

With that, she excused herself to the kitchen to prepare a late lunch for her Hacks. She shed tears while she worked, but smiled as she shed them. They were not tears of loss, but of completion, because she was giving Rich the best farewell she knew how.

Ryan had several tasks on his radar, getting Heather alone to discuss possible limited editions of her backlist among them, but they were busy signing sheets, inscribing books Susan had brought along, and then exchanging books they themselves had packed for each other to sign. Heather's pen was getting the best workout. The others, including, to his surprise, Casper, had brought their own copies of many of her books. It didn't look like any of these well-respected genre writers thought of her as a hack. But that didn't surprise Ryan, who had always thought her work to be unpretentious, even fun. Two qualities sorely lacking in a field where too many took themselves too seriously.

Ryan had his own books to get signed, but that could wait. They had the whole week. Leaving the roomful of Hacks to their signing and trading, he slipped away to the kitchen to see if Susan needed any help.

Funny, he thought. Susan had more money than most of the Hacks would ever see, but would not even consider bringing help to take care of the cooking and cleaning.

"Susan, could you use an extra hand?"

He turned into the kitchen and stopped.

Susan stood at the counter, slicing tomatoes and arranging them on a platter full of finger foods, crackers, cheese, chips, and a bowl of dip, sandwich meats, and bread. Bacon and hamburgers cooked over the blue flames of the gas stove.

She was crying while she worked. She seemed not to have heard Ryan.

He backed away to give the distraught woman some privacy, turned and started back to the main room, where he heard Camp talking to Bill, pointing toward the white Jeep and asking, "Who is that creepy fuck anyway?"

"Yahoo the Swedish Meatball," Bill said with a chuckle.

Ryan peered at Yohan through the front window, still sitting in his Jeep, still watching the gathered writers with a kind of blank contempt.

The sooner we get rid of him, the better, Ryan thought, remembering the watcher in the woods, the man who had tracked him through the trees, but would not show himself.

Remembering the beheaded bear, not old as he had told the others, but fresh.

He wanted that creepy fuck out of there.

CHAPTER 8

Misery by Firelight

Jim could have told Susan not to worry too much about the food. Every writer at one time or another in their life has existed on a mac & cheese or Ramen diet. Most are not picky eaters. On the contrary, most are just happy to have something to eat.

Susan brought the platter out. Sandwiches and burgers were quickly assembled and eaten, the finger foods vanished soon after, and by the end of the afternoon, everyone seemed happy and sated.

As the excitement wound down, conversation eased from a free-for-all frenzy to a relaxed trading of stories and discussions of favorite books, movies, and writers.

That was always how it worked. Whenever writers got together, the first serious topics consisted of their influences and favorites. They seemed to gauge each other that way, almost to judge each other.

Jim seriously considered listing J.K. Rowling and her Harry Potter books as one of his favorites, they were, but decided it would be safer to leave them out. Later,

Michael admitted to enjoying the Twilight books, and was repaid with blank stares and a few polite coughs.

As the sun fell, Susan showed them to their individual cabins. Ryan used a second room in the lodge, and Bill and Camp were sharing a cabin, but the others had cabins of their own.

Later, after all had settled into their cabins, the Hacks gathered outside to continue their camp-warming party, where they would catch what was shaping up to be a magnificent sunset.

The Department of Lands crew had set logs, stripped of bark and flattened to approximate benches. They circled the stone fire pit, tree stump chairs set in pairs between them. Bill and Camp carried the easy chair outside, displacing two tree stump chairs to accommodate Casper's bad back.

Bill, Ryan, Susan, and Tracy had brought cameras, and took pictures of the sunset, bruised-purple clouds set against a fire-orange western horizon. They promised the others to send copies.

The sun took its final bow behind Mount Misery's western peaks, the day's residual heat dissipated, and Ryan volunteered to start a fire.

"Jim, mind helping with the wood?"

"Yeah," Jim said. "Anybody bring hot dogs and marsh-mallows?"

Susan had, and went to fetch them while Ryan and Jim went for wood.

As they left the artificial light thrown through the lodge's windows, Jim fully appreciated how isolated The Devil's Tail Ridge was. He hoped they wouldn't have to walk too far.

"Just around here," Ryan said, motioning around the far side of the lodge.

Jim could just barely make out two large mounds of stacked wood behind the building.

"Stick out your arms and I'll load you up."

Jim held out his arms, and Ryan stacked wood on them. "What do you think of Heather?"

The question caught Jim off guard.

After a moment's hesitation, he said, "She's okay. Very nice, actually."

Ryan grunted a reply, and Jim saw a faint glimmer of white in the starlight as Ryan smiled. "I notice you're not wearing a wedding ring anymore. Tan line's almost gone too."

Jim sighed. "With any luck Shelly will be gone by the time I get home."

"Sorry to hear that."

"I'm not," Jim said, a little harshly, he realized. "We weren't suited for each other." He staggered forward as Ryan dropped more wood into his outstretched arms. "I'm about full."

"Okay. Give me a second." Ryan filled one arm with nearly as much wood as Jim held in both of his. "So, you rode up with Heather, right?"

"Yeah. Flew in with her too, but I didn't know it was her until we'd landed."

"What do you think of her?" Ryan topped his load of firewood off with a small grunt, fumbled around the wood stack for a moment, finally finding the handle of an axe that that was leaning against it.

"I don't know," Jim said, blushing a little, wondering

why Ryan was grilling him. Was it that obvious that he was taken with her?

"I'm going to try and reprint her first few books," Ryan said. "Limited edition, thinking a thousand copies each."

"Ah," Jim said and smiled. *That's his angle.* "You'd sure as hell sell them. If you can get the rights."

"I wasn't sure if she'd take me seriously, but she seemed impressed with the small press editions Susan brought."

"She knows the small press," Jim said. "She has a copy of my collection." The collection was the first of Jim's books that Ryan published.

"Really." Ryan said, sounding pleased. "I'll have to ask her what she thinks of it."

Jim followed Ryan back around the side of the lodge. "If it comes to it, I'll put in a good word for you."

"I may hold you to that," Ryan said. "For now, mum's the word."

They rounded the corner, stepping back into the lodge's gas light.

Jim relaxed as the darkness fell away. He hadn't realized how oppressive it had been until he was out of it.

They dropped their loads of wood behind Ryan's stump, and Ryan began to split some of the wood into kindling.

By the time Susan returned with a cooler of hot dogs and marshmallows, Ryan had constructed a kindling house, a halfway decent miniature of the lodge Jim thought, and lit it up.

The kindling house burned quickly, and after it collapsed, Ryan stacked thicker chunks of wood on top and around it. While Susan fed hot dogs onto extendible forks and passed them around, the small fire became a blaze.

Light and heat enveloped the gathered wordsmiths.

Heather made Jim blush by feeding him a burnt hot dog from the end of her fork. Casper passed on the marshmallows, citing high blood sugar. Michael looked increasingly uncomfortable with the special attention Tracy was paying him, having sidled up so close she was almost in his lap, right arm curled behind his back. Bill and Camp cracked everybody up with a theatric reenactment of a bonfire party they'd started in the parking lot of a Baltimore hotel at a convention a few years before.

Heather laughed when Jim tried to force feed her a roasted marshmallow.

Susan remained silent, seemed content to let her Hacks amuse themselves for the time being.

The moon came up, very large and very bright from where they sat.

Ryan told a spooky story about a camping trip into the wilderness by his childhood home. Jim wondered, glancing into the dark that surrounded them, if any of it was true.

"I have one," Bill said, standing up, stretching his arms. He rolled his head, and Heather flinched a little as his spine crackled.

"This is a true story," he said, his face suddenly serious. He kept the solemn, businesslike expression as he recounted the story of Yahoo The Swedish Meatball and his torrid love affair with Harry The Headless Bear.

Where the hell *is* Yahoo, Jim wondered. He'd managed to forget about their guide during the good time following his near blowup, but thinking back, didn't remember him leaving.

Hoping he wasn't somewhere close, listening, Jim scanned the landing around the lodge. He saw Camp's Mustang, but not the Jeep.

He gave up his search after a few moments, and listened, laughing, as Bill's story came to its ridiculous conclusion.

Casper excused himself, retiring to his cabin, and in the half hour following, Susan, Ryan, Michael, and then Tracy followed suit.

When Tracy's cabin door thumped shut, Camp shook his head.

"That woman is on a mission," he said. "I wonder how far down Michael's pants she'll crawl before she finds out he's gay?"

Bill laughed.

Again, Jim wasn't sure how to take the comment, so he only smiled politely.

Beside him, almost leaning into him, Heather gave a low moan.

"He's watching," she said. "He's going to be mad."

Jim recognized the slow, despairing tone from her spell during the limo ride.

"Who's watching?" Bill stood and moved closer to them.

Camp's hand moved, as if by instinct, toward the gun in his Cover Your Ass holster.

Jim shook his head at them, then gave Heather a little shake. "Heather, wake up."

She stiffened in his arm, then let out a long exhale.

Her eyes turned to him, confused for a moment, then she relaxed.

"Oh, sorry. I must have drifted off." Again, she sounded embarrassed, almost ashamed. She rose and stretched. "Think I'll call it a night."

She walked briskly toward her cabin.

"Wait up," Jim said. "I'm going to turn in too. I'll walk with you."

"Thanks," she said, but didn't slow her pace.

"Nite, guys," Jim said.

They nodded in return, Bill asking, "Is she okay?"

Jim shrugged and turned to follow Heather. He caught up to her at her cabin, the second to last on the far side of the lodge. His was the last.

"I didn't embarrass myself too badly, did I?" she asked, turning to Jim as he slowed his pace beside her.

"No, not at all."

"What did I say this time?"

"You said *he* was watching. That he was going to be mad."

"Oh," she said but did not elaborate.

"Who is *he*?"

No answer.

"Heather?"

She stopped at her doorway and turned to him.

"Jim, I like you. Quite a lot," she added with a small laugh that was almost a sob. "But I'd rather not talk about this now."

"That's fine, but if there is anything I can do …"

"I'll keep that in mind," she interrupted him. Then she took his hands in hers. "I'm glad you're here. Thanks."

She smiled, dropped his hands, and before he could speak again, disappeared inside her cabin.

Jim went to his own cabin and closed his door against the cool mountain air. The heater had already kicked in, and the warmth made him sleepy. He kicked off his shoes, crawled into his bed, and fell sleep with Heather's smiling face still on his mind.

Heather did not sleep. She lay awake, thinking about *him*.

He's watching.

She was sure of it, even up here in the mountains a thousand miles from home. Watching, waiting for her to be alone again. He'd finally figured it out, and he was on her trail again. She was stupid to think she could run.

She wished she'd brought her gun, but there was no way to get it through airport security. Maybe he had it with him now, wherever he was.

There was a sound from outside. Just one of a thousand noises of the wild, but to Heather it was the sound of *him*, standing at the window at the back of her cabin, staring in.

Or maybe it was Yohan.

Yohan reminded her of him, a lot.

Maybe Yohan was working for him. Maybe he had found out her plans and come ahead of her. Crazy as it sounded, it was the kind of thing he would do.

Anyone else would have given up by now. It had been

six years since her last close call with him, a chance sighting on the road.

The last few years had been a nightmare of constant worry, the price for her unexpected success.

The sound came again. It might have been a squirrel climbing the side of her cabin, a robin pecking the ground for its late-night snack, or him, standing in the dark beneath her window, watching her. Making her sweat before he finally came around to her door.

If she'd thought by leaving him all those years ago, that she was finally out of his shadow, she'd been wrong.

She'd never left it. His shadow had followed her. She felt it now, even if she couldn't see it in the solid blackness of her cabin.

Snap out of it you ditzy bitch! The only reason you came was to get away from him. No one knows you're here.

She worked up what courage she had left, pushed her blankets aside and sat up, almost expecting to feel his hands on her exposed throat, and turned toward the window behind her.

For a second, she actually saw him there, a silhouette backlit by a sliver of moon that had broken through the trees. Her breathing stopped, and there was a moment when she thought the fear would kill her. Then she blinked, and the watcher at her window was gone.

Never there, she thought. *He's a thousand miles away, maybe standing outside my empty bedroom. Watching, but not seeing. Waiting a thousand miles away.*

A burst of laughter out front shattered the almost perfect silence. Heather slapped a hand over her mouth to keep from crying out.

It was Camp. He and Bill were still out there. Surely if

there were someone snooping around, Bill and Camp would have heard them.

Heather fought a sudden urge to go to Jim's cabin and knock until he let her in.

He's going to be mad.

Bastard, she thought, and cried.

She remembered the letter, *his* letter, folded at the bottom of her bag. She wanted nothing more than to tear it up and burn it, scatter the ashes. She needed to keep it though, just in case he did find her. So the police would know it was him.

He'd finally found out where she was, who she was, and he was coming for her. This time, his note promised, she would not get away.

When Heather did sleep, he was waiting for her in her dreams.

"Bless you, Camp," Bill said, twisting the top off his second bottle of Smirnoff. He tipped the bottle back and made it half empty. Feeling a slight buzz now, he resolved to cut himself off at two.

Camp on the other hand, was downing his third cup of hobo coffee, boiled over the coals of their dying fire. Nasty stuff, gritty and too strong. Camp didn't touch alcohol. Coffee, gallons of it a day, was the catalyst of Camp's wild, bug-eyed personality. Every few gulps, he would spit out the wet grounds. Only after he'd sucked out the extra caffeine though.

"Any idea what the Hack-Master has planned for us?"

"Not a clue," Bill said, nursing the second half of his

second bottle. Making it last. "You should ask Ryan. He's probably planned most of it."

Camp jumped up, sloshing his tin mug of hobo-coffee onto his lap and cussing. "Gotta wizz," he said, and walked toward the canyon edge.

"Toilets the other way, dumbass."

"Fuck that," Camp said. "I've never pissed into a canyon before."

"Don't fall in," Bill said, and began to giggle. Slightly buzzed had slipped easily into nicely buzzed. A third, he reasoned, would put him over the top.

No, he'd promised Susan he wouldn't do that. She'd given him permission to drink, not that he needed it, but he'd promised not to get rip-roaring drunk. And he'd promised not to drink at all in front of Casper. H Casper was a legendary drunk in his earlier years, but age and health had forced him to leave that behind.

Bill respected that. Camp had been faced with such a choice once, and had made the right choice. Too many blackout rages, too many mornings waking in strange beds with stranger women, and too many dates with the gutter and the toilet bowl. Too many close calls.

Of course, with Camp, drugs had been involved too. Pills mostly. That had started with the accident at Camp's shop, when his shirt sleeve had caught in the fan belt of a running engine. When they'd finally untangled him from the belts and wheels, his right hand had been nearly torn off. Only a few inches of flesh and grizzle had held it on. A year of therapy had given him back as much use as he would ever get out of it, but he could still turn a wrench and fire a gun.

Camp had taken to calling his scarred right hand

Frankenhand, stitch-work scars circled the wrist and ran up the palm to his middle finger. The tip of that was gone, and the knuckle would forever be stiff and unbending.

Camp had become adept at hiding it around people he didn't know, keeping it tucked away in a pocket, or hidden beneath crossed arms, but once the others had gone to their cabins, out it came. Camp turned it over and studied, like a man studying a road map.

"I don't mind Frankenhand too much," Camp had once confided in Bill. "It's cool for a laugh now and then."

Camp had once made an editor they didn't like run drunk and screaming from a party by wiggling it in her face and groaning like a B-movie monster.

"Biggest adjustment," he'd said in all seriousness, "is learning to jack off left handed. I keep on spraining my wrist."

"Hey."

Bill turned his head and found Tracy emerging from the darkness by the cluster of cabins.

She looked pissed.

Bill nodded, and offered her a bottle from the cooler by his tree stump seat. "What's up?"

"Have you guys been around the cabins?"

"Nope. Been here all night."

"Oh." She looked confused for a moment, then shrugged and twisted the cap off her bottle. "Heard someone outside my cabin," she explained. "Thought it was Michael, so I went to ask him what he wanted."

Bill had to bite his lip not to laugh.

Tracy spied Camp's coffee makings and sat down on the log bench next to them. "Where's Camp?"

Bill motioned toward the canyon. "Taking a leak. Should be back in a minute."

"Oh, okay." She tipped her bottle back and sucked greedily. She tipped the bottle toward him and said, "Thanks."

"No problem."

"Anyway, I went to Michael's cabin to see what he wanted." She sounded supremely offended. "He got pissed and kicked me out."

"Guess it wasn't him you heard then," Bill said, unable to stop the smile now.

Tracy seemed not to notice, or care. She shrugged, as if to say *who fucking cares? That's not the point.*

"Wonder what his problem was anyway?" Her lips made sexy pouting shapes between sips of her Smirnoff.

"Don't take it too personally," Camp said, returning to the glow of the low burning fire. He zipped up with his left hand, held his right just out of sight behind his leg. Then he dropped down beside her, slipping his right arm easily around Tracy's waist, the stiff middle finger of Frankenhand brushing her breast. He tipped Bill a sly little wink as he did it.

Tracy smirked, and put a not so subtle hand on Camp's thigh.

Bill drained his bottle, tossed it back into the cooler, and rose. "I'm outa' here, kids. Be good."

Tracy, whose full attention was now on Camp, ignored Bill.

Camp chugged the remaining coffee in his cup and said, "I won't do anything you wouldn't."

Walking back to his cabin, leaving the heat of the fire

behind, the chill began to beat down Bill's comfortable buzz.

He wondered if Tracy was lying about hearing someone snooping behind her cabin, and if not, who that someone might have been.

Ryan hadn't really been sleepy, he'd been having far too much fun, but he wanted to rise early. He'd set his alarm to rise with the sun, and his fishing rod and tackle box were ready beside his night stand. With any luck, he'd catch enough of those trout to make breakfast for the lot of them.

Though he wasn't sleepy when he started for his room on the second story of the lodge, it came quickly. It was the sounds of nature, the whisper of the wind, the song of birds and crickets. He'd opened his window before turning off his gas lamp and lying down.

The smell of mountain air, crisp and clean and spiced with pine and wildflower.

Someone should bottle this smell, he thought, right before drifting away.

But he woke with another scent. Something foul and unwashed and rotting. Like that bear's corpse had smelled. It washed through his window, through his room.

"God damn," he said, and stood to close his window. As he reached for it, he heard the sound of falling wood. Someone behind the lodge. He moved slowly, inching his face toward the open window, then angling it out, looking down.

Someone was down there. A very large someone. The man moved into a slightly lighter shade of darkness, and Ryan drew back instinctively, not wanting to be seen. For a moment he thought he'd been looking down at a bear. But it was not a bear, just a man in a filthy fur coat and hat.

He thought of Yohan instantly, and the heat of anger rose in him.

"Hey, you!" Ryan shouted, not caring if he was seen now.

With a grunt of surprise, the man below bolted into the woods.

"Son of a bitch."

Ryan pulled a shirt over his head and slipped into his shoes, then navigated his way through the dark lodge as quickly as he could.

Bill met him outside, stumbling in the dark and rubbing sleep from his eyes. "What's the noise about?"

Ryan put a finger to his lips, and sprinted to Bill's side, whispering, "Someone's snooping around behind the cabins."

Bill grabbed Ryan's arm. He was alert now, eyes narrowed. "Tracy said she heard someone outside her cabin earlier."

"Yohan," Ryan said, shaking off Bill's hand and walking back to the lodge, then behind it.

Bill followed.

No one waited for them. Ryan headed for the trees, but Bill stopped him.

"Not now," he said. "You scared him away. We'll deal with it tomorrow."

Ryan nodded.

"Talk to Camp tomorrow morning. Let him know what's going on. I'll talk to Jim. I know the area well enough, as long as no one wanders down into the canyon." They stopped at the fire ring and Ryan sat down. "You think Camp would mind running people to the airport when the week is over?"

"I'll ask him, but I don't think he'd mind." He patted Ryan on the back. "Sit tight for a second."

Then he left Ryan, walking toward Camp's Mustang.

Ryan watched his progress through the dark, then turned his face toward the corpse of last night's fire. A few small coals still glowed, sending up weak puffs of smoke, but it was mostly dead now. Cold.

Bill returned a minute later with two cold bottles of Smirnoff.

"Don't worry," Bill said, handing one to Ryan. "I'm keeping myself in check. Casper won't ever know I have them here."

"Thanks," Ryan said, twisting the cap off and taking a drink.

"Thank Camp," Bill said, smiling and tipping his bottle back. He took a long swallow, sighed, and said, "The man's a real-life Boy Scout."

They spent the next half hour nursing their drinks and working out a gentle, but persuasive argument for getting rid of Yohan.

They only hoped Susan would agree.

CHAPTER 10

Conspirators

Jim woke to knocking on his cabin door, and felt a moment of disorientation when he opened his eyes. It happened whenever he slept, or woke, in a strange place. The knock came again, then a voice.

"Jim, get your lazy ass out of bed and come fishing with me."

Ryan.

"Give me a minute," Jim shouted, and groaned as his customary morning headache gave a nasty throb. "Shit."

He levered his legs off the narrow bed and sat up, slipping his bare feet into the shoes he'd left beside it. He felt like a slob, meeting his publisher, a man with whom his relationship had always been very professional, unwashed, hair sticking up in every grease stiffened direction, in the pants he'd slept in.

Jim unlocked his cabin door and opened it, gasping at the cool breeze that embraced him. It felt good though.

"Can it wait until I shower?"

"If you have to, but be quick." Jim had to step aside as he rushed in. "Coffee?"

Ryan held up a thermos. Two coffee mugs clanked together, hanging by their handles from fingers of the same hand.

"I'd love some," Jim said, grimacing again at another throb from his aching head.

Jim felt a little uncomfortable undressing in the same room with Ryan, only a half partition separating him from the rest of the one room cabin, but Ryan paid him no mind. He set his fishing rod and tackle box against the door beside the wall, then sat at the small, central table with his thermos.

The shower was quick, the water pressure almost nonexistent, but the water was good and hot. Jim knew he was lucky to have that much where they were. He dried off and dressed in clean clothes he'd stacked on the stool beside the shower.

A steaming mug of coffee awaited him at the table. He sat down next to Ryan, sipped at his coffee, found it wonderful, and gulped it down. When the cup was empty, Ryan refilled it.

"Didn't think we were allowed to fish on Department of Lands land."

"Oh yeah," Ryan said. "It's legal. The out-of-state license cost me a small fortune though. Figure since I spent your next advance on it, I might as well bring you along."

Jim laughed.

"You think I'm kidding, do you?"

"God, I hope you are."

Ryan shrugged but said no more until they'd finished the thermos.

"Off we go." Ryan led the way out into the cool, dark morning. The glow on the horizon was only a promise of true light. The glow that preceded the sun.

Jim had found the place spooky at night, but the light, even the weak light of early morning, revealed a different world.

I could live here, Jim thought, knowing he damn well could not. *Great place to visit, but you wouldn't want to live here. Jim could survive a week without electricity and television and the Internet, but two weeks? A month? Naw.*

Ryan led them at a brisk pace down the trail toward the lake. This time Jim had more time to appreciate the sights along the way.

"Are those huckleberries?" Jim had seen them in pictures, but never first hand. He resisted an urge to bend and pluck one from the bush until he had an affirmative from Ryan.

"Not those," Ryan said. "Don't want to eat those."

"Poisonous?"

"Nope," Ryan said. "But they taste nasty, and they'll give you the screaming shits if you eat more than a few."

"I'll take your word for it," Jim said, giving the bush a last look, marking it before he moved again.

They passed the outhouse, Jim was glad that he had a real toilet back in his cabin, and Ryan stopped at the first narrow trail into the woods. The one Jim had searched yesterday, looking for footprints, scraps of cloth hanging from thorns or broken limbs, blood. Ryan narrowed his eyes and leaned forward into the mouth of the trail.

Then he smiled and set his fishing rod and box down. "This way."

Jim followed him reluctantly. A few feet in, Ryan crouched, and pointed.

"This," he said, turning his grin toward Jim, "is a huckleberry bush."

He plucked a few plump, purple berries and tossed them into his open mouth.

Ryan did the same. "Delicious," he said.

"We can bring a few buckets later and pick some."

A few minutes hike away, they found the granite slab Ryan had knelt on while washing the cut on his head. The bandage was gone now and the cut seemed to have closed up nicely.

Ryan set his rod down, then flipped the latch on his tackle box. Instead of the jar of fish eggs or the lures Jim had expected, Ryan brought out a small hatchet and what Jim thought of as a Boy Scout knife. Equipped with multiple blades and tools, it folded out into a pair of needle nose pliers. Ryan handed Jim the hatchet and pulled up a long, serrated blade. He then surprised Jim by marching back up the bank to the trail, toward the dead bear path.

"Hack off a few of the larger limbs," Ryan said, pointing in the general direction of the woods.

"Why?"

"Camouflage," Ryan said, and Jim understood.

They worked until the sun was up, shining down on the mirrored surface of the lake, then arranged their harvest of limbs, and a few stunted trees in front of the trail. When they were finished it was as close to invisible as they could make it.

"There," Ryan said, wiping a trickle of sweat from his forehead. "Now we don't have to worry about someone else taking that trail and getting the same scare I did."

Jim nodded. "Good idea."

"Let's have a seat," Ryan said as they walked back toward the lake. "We need to talk."

"Yohan," Jim said, his cheeks flushing bright red. "You think it was him?"

Ryan had shared his and Bill's suspicions, the person who'd stalked Ryan through the trees the day before as he explored, the person Tracy claimed to have heard creeping around her cabin the night before, the person Ryan had *seen* creeping around behind the lodge.

Ryan didn't mention the decapitated bear. A fresh corpse. He was mildly freaked out about that. A bear was not a human though, and a poacher was not a murderer. The others, however, were likely to make more out of it than was really there. It's what writers did.

"Who else?" Ryan said, reeling his line in. "No one knows we're here besides the Department of Lands. Susan hasn't told anyone but us about it." Ryan checked the hook. Satisfied with the cover of eggs still impaled on the hook, he tossed it back in. The bobber splashed water up, then rode a lazy breeze toward the center of the lake. "Besides, I have a feeling it's the kind of thing Yahoo would get a kick out of."

"Yeah," Jim said. "I get that feeling too. So, what now?"

"We convince Susan we don't need him. Shouldn't be hard. I know she doesn't like him. We don't stray any farther than this lake," he said. "We know the trails well enough, and we know to keep the others away from that one." He hooked a thumb back over his shoulder toward the concealed trail.

Jim nodded.

"Bill is going to ask Camp about giving us all rides back to the airport."

"Good," Jim said. He'd risen and paced around the granite slab. "No need to tell everyone else I suppose?"

"No," Ryan said. "We'll be with Susan when she lets him go. If there's any problem the four of us can handle it."

"Thank God for Camp and his gun," Jim said.

Ryan agreed. He didn't think it would come to that, but still...

———

When Jim and Ryan arrived back at the lodge, everyone else was awake, wandering around in varying states of awareness. Jim searched for Bill and Camp, then located them standing at the door of their cabin, Camp sucking down a mug of coffee like it was oxygen.

He caught Bill's eye, and gave him a conspiratorial little nod as they walked his way.

"Good morning, Jim."

Jim saw Heather standing at the door of her cabin, looking even better than he had remembered her. Her hair was wet and uncombed.

"Hey," Jim said, and felt better about the morning. His nervousness about the coming business with Yohan seemed to lessen. "Sleep well?"

Heather shook her head. "Not really. I don't do well in strange places." She yawned, then cast a nervous glance toward the woods behind her cabin.

"Had a nightmare. Dreamed that someone was watching me while I slept. It felt so real too. For a second I actually saw someone standing at my window." She laughed then, but it sounded forced to Jim. "Probably Just being silly."

He caught the quick sidelong glance Ryan threw him.

"Not really," Jim said. "I'm the same way."

"Want to come in for coffee?"

The invitation caught Jim off guard, and he paused his steady pace toward the lodge. Ryan stopped beside him, waiting.

"Yeah," Jim said, and again felt his spirits rise a bit. "I'll be a few minutes though. You mind waiting for me?"

"You know where I am," Heather said, smiling as she disappeared back into her cabin.

Jim and Ryan fell into pace beside Bill and Camp on their way to the lodge, and it occurred to Jim that the four of them must look ridiculously like something out of a spaghetti western. Adding to the sense of unreality, the distant screech of an eagle, and an answering echo in the canyon.

"Let's do this," Bill said as they crossed the porch to the lodge's front door.

"Let me talk to her, okay? Back me up if I need it, but I don't think I will."

The others said nothing, and paused at the door to let

Ryan lead them in. They found Susan in the kitchen, cooking bacon, eggs, and hash browns over the flames of the large stove's dozen burners. Enough to feed a small army.

Ryan stopped just inside the kitchen and said, "Susan, we have to talk."

Susan had a feeling she knew what this was about, but was startled to see half of her Hacks standing behind Ryan.

"Let me help," Camp said, stepping up and smoothly taking over the flipping of bacon. Jim took over the eggs and hash browns, and Ryan pulled a seat out at the table, motioning for Susan to sit.

Bill kept his place in the doorway between hallway and kitchen, like a guard. He pointed to the two-way radio on the table. "That work?"

"Yes," Susan said. "It's battery operated so I don't leave it on."

Bill nodded, seeming satisfied.

"Susan, the Yohan situation is getting out of hand."

She listened, her insides going ice cold as Ryan told her about the man who'd stalked him through the woods right after Yohan had dropped Heather and Jim off. Susan knew the timing was right, Yohan could have parked down the road and hiked through the woods to where Ryan was. Yohan knew The Devil's Tail like the back of his hand. His own words to her.

The ice in her chest melted when Ryan told her about their peeping tom.

Bastard, she thought. Then she slammed a fist on the table, making them all jump. "Bastard!"

"There's no way we can prove it," Ryan said. "But you don't need proof to let him go. In fact, it might be better if we didn't mention any of this to him. Just tell him you don't need his services anymore."

A part of Susan wanted to scream *bullshit*, to call Yohan out, expose him. Embarrass him. She knew Ryan was right though. The less conflict, the better. Just send him away and salvage the rest of their time.

Most important was that the others, Heather and Tracy especially, didn't find out. It would ruin the experience for them. If they spent the whole retreat looking over their shoulders, unable to sleep at night, Susan would never be able to forgive herself.

"Okay," she said at last.

Ryan sighed. Seemed relieved.

Susan was not. She still had Yohan to deal with.

"He'll be here soon," Susan said. "I'll wait until breakfast is over and call him in here."

Ryan shook his head, and behind her Bill said, "We're not going to make you do this yourself, Susan."

"Can we move breakfast outside?" Jim asked. "If we can get everyone else away from the lodge we won't need to wait."

"We can do it right here. It's your show," Ryan hastened to add when Susan turned back to him. "We'll let you handle him if you want, but I know he won't try anything with the four of us standing behind you."

Susan nodded. "There's an extra table in the utility room. We can move it outside for breakfast."

Jim and Camp had finished cooking breakfast, and were dishing it onto plates.

"There a coffee pot here?" Camp asked.

"Yes, I'll make it." Then, "Thank you, guys. I appreciate your help."

"No problem," Bill said. "That's what Hacks are for."

Jim didn't get to have his coffee with Heather after all. Yohan's white Jeep tore into the clearing as the four of them helped Susan carry plates to the table outside. The morning dew kept his tires from kicking up dust, but they did throw gravel as he pulled a sharp turn and skidded to a stop beside the lodge.

Susan ignored him until they'd set the plates on the table, and then called the others over. "Go ahead and start without us. We'll be out in a few minutes."

Heather shot Jim a pout as she sat down, but he sensed a smile underneath, ready to break through.

"Rain check?" he asked

Heather sighed. "Okay, but I expect you to make it up to me."

While Jim started back to the lodge, the others ahead of him, Susan was talking to Yohan, who nodded sharply and stalked in ahead of her.

Yohan, Bill noted, was not a man who took rejection well. He argued and questioned. Accused her of wasting his time and insisted she would pay for a full week of his services, since he'd turned down other jobs to be there.

Bill doubted that, but kept his mouth shut.

Susan stuck to her guns. She wrote him a check that more than covered his few days of work and told him to take it or leave it.

Yohan looked on the edge of rage, but he finally took the check and stalked out of the kitchen.

Bill, Camp, Ryan, and Jim followed.

Bill thought Yohan might kick up a storm with the others outside, maybe leave a few parting shots in hopes of spoiling their day, but he didn't. He walked straight for his Jeep, not even looking at them.

And just when it seemed it would end without any real trouble, Michael spoke up.

"Hey, Yahoo! Not staying for breakfast?"

Bill groaned. Behind him, Ryan cursed.

Michael, having realized his slip, blushed, then went white as Yohan turned and charged at him.

"My name is *Yohan*, you cocky little shit!"

Bill ran, the others close behind, but Yohan reached the table first.

Michael seemed frozen to his seat, looking on in stunned disbelief as Yohan drew back a balled-up fist.

Casper seemed to come from nowhere. Standing next to Yohan, his large fist arching down, landing solidly on Yohan's jaw and putting him on his ass.

Yohan stared up at Casper in utter disbelief.

"You big tub of shit," he said, almost gasped, but before he could find his feet, Bill and Jim had him by the arms and began dragging him away.

The rage that had lurked just beneath the surface in

the lodge's kitchen broke loose. Yohan cursed and kicked at them, but only made it worse for himself as he stumbled and fell again and again on his trip back to the Jeep. Ryan had stayed behind with Casper, but Camp followed a few feet behind.

Bill half expected to see his gun in hand, but it was not. Not yet, anyway.

"Let me go you son's-a-bitches!"

And they did, shoving him into his Jeep and stepping back.

Yohan made a move toward them, but seemed to think better of it when neither man backed off.

"Listen, douchebag," Bill said, dangerously close to losing what remained of his self-control. "This is your one and only chance to get out of here without a broken head."

Camp was beside them now, grinning cheerily.

Yohan backed off a step, ass bumping into the door of his Jeep.

"If you come back, I won't bother with you. I'll just give you to Camp."

Camp's smile broadened.

Without another word, Yohan climbed into his Jeep and backed up. A moment later he disappeared down The Devil's Tail.

They started back toward the lodge. Bill noticed Jim starting to shake. Belated fear or unspent adrenaline, he wasn't sure which.

"I had no idea it would be this much fun," Camp said. "I hope she invites me back next year."

Making Friends

Casper finished his breakfast one-handed while Susan iced, then wrapped his swollen hand.

"Been a few years since I've done anything like that," Casper said, and actually laughed. For the first time since arriving he seemed energized, interested in the goings on around him.

Michael spent the rest of the morning in orbit around Casper, thanking him a hundred times, at least, and doing every small thing for him that Casper would allow.

"Don't stop suddenly, H. We'll have to pull him out by his ankles," Camp said to Casper as they all walked back to the lodge after breakfast was cleared away.

When Casper did stop, turning to respond, Michael ran into him and almost fell down. Everyone got a laugh out of it, including Casper and Michael, but Michael also blushed a bright red, and kept his distance afterward.

Susan seemed to have recovered from the blowup with Yohan, even seemed less strained as she gathered them into the lodge's main room and asked them all to read something from one of the books she'd brought, or if they were comfortable, sharing one of their works in progress.

Heather was first, reading the opening chapter from a newly completed novel. Bill and Camp went next, doing a comedic dramatization of a coauthored short story about a family of redneck zombies. Michael read an original short story, a ghost story that had half of them in tears by the time he was finished. Tracy read the opening chapter of her new novel, a sizzler that left half the party blushing, and the other half hyperventilating.

When Jim took the floor, he came very close to freezing up. He didn't like public speaking of any kind, and opening up an untested and unproven story to public criticism seemed especially daunting.

Heather's reassuring smile helped … a little.

He read from a stack of wrinkled, typewritten pages. The prologue to the novel he was having such a hard time finishing. The reading took five minutes, and he only stumbled a few times.

When Jim finished, Ryan stood and announced the publication date, as he was publishing the first limited hardcover edition. "That is, if he manages to complete it."

There were a few polite laughs, and Jim blushed.

Then Casper made his day by saying, "Well, I hope you do. That was quite good. I'm curious to see where you're going with it."

On that note, the morning reading ended, and the Hacks scattered, some to separate corners of the lodge, some outside, and others to their cabins.

Heather went straight to Jim.

"Time to cash in on that rain check," she said, and took him by the arm.

Bill watched Heather drag Jim toward the door, and shook his head.

Lucky bastard, he thought.

Already people were hooking up. First Camp and Tracy, now Jim and Heather. Just like any other convention the numbers favored the women. Unlike usual, his contingent of fans, at least half of them women, was not there. He missed them now. The signing of breasts and other body parts was his favorite convention pastime.

Oh well, he thought. *That's not what Hacks was about anyway.* Also, it was much easier to stay faithful to Lacy when the mob Camp had dubbed the Femme Fatales wasn't on his heels.

Thinking about Lacy brought a smile.

Bill worried when he got his invitation, that she either wouldn't want him to go, or worse, that she would let him, but would pout and play the wounded wife until he left.

She had done neither. She'd been excited for him, and had *insisted* that he go.

Bill missed his fans, but more than that, he missed Lacy, his wife and number one fan.

"Yo, Bill."

Camp's shout startled Bill from his thoughts, and he saw his friend approaching with Tracy by his side and his prized Jets cap on her head. He was mildly surprised to find Camp still apparently interested in Tracy after having already *nailed her,* as Camp had put it this morning. Bill supposed if she was half as wild in the sheets as she was on the page, it made sense.

"We're going to take a dip at the lake," Tracy said. "You coming?"

"Why not," Bill said.

"Michael," Camp said. "Come to the lake with us."

Bill wondered if this was Camp's way of making peace after embarrassing him.

Michael, who had his face stuck in a copy of Cemetery Dance, looked startled for a moment, then said, "Yeah, sure."

Ryan found Susan standing alone at the edge of the canyon.

He thought she might be crying again, but decided not to leave her this time. He'd been able to help her through much of her grief after Rich had died, and she had seemed to welcome that help. If there was anything he could do now, he would. He loathed the thought of her spending what should be a good time isolated by her lingering grief.

"Susan," he said as he approached her, not wanting to startle her while she stood so close to the edge.

She turned, and he saw her face was calm, peaceful. Not crying. She gave him a smile, a curious turn of her head, then waved him over. She sat in the grass as he drew near, and he sat next to her.

"I just knew Yohan was going to ruin the whole week, but I was afraid to fire him. Not so much afraid *of* him," she added, and Ryan knew that was not the whole truth. She had been scared of him. "I just didn't trust myself to be able to do this without his help."

She laughed.

"Maybe I was frightened I'd lose you all in the woods."

"Susan …," he started, but she held up a hand and silenced him.

She was quiet for a moment, staring out into the great open space.

Ryan saw a line of blue at the bottom of the canyon. A narrow river. He wondered how many thousands of years it had taken that river to carve the canyon before them.

"I think I was just afraid of doing it alone. I guess I was too thick to realize I was never alone." She took his hand, squeezed it and let it go. "Thank you."

"I am happy to help," Ryan said.

"I know you are," she said, and gave him another curious sideways glance. "I've known for a while."

Oh shit, Ryan thought.

This was not what he wanted, her thinking of him as some kind of vulture, an opportunistic prick drawn to the scent of a wealthy woman's grief.

"It's okay," she assured him, as if reading his mind. "I know you're not a gold digger."

Then she shocked him by cupping a hand behind his head and drawing him close, pressing her lips to his.

Then she released him and said, "I'm glad that happened. It's been almost a year now, and I've been very lonely."

Jim sat across the table from Heather, behind the closed door of her cabin, not drinking coffee, but talking. Idle talk, about nothing. Flirting. At one point he realized he might be coming on a little strong, and backed off. He wasn't even divorced yet, not until he returned home to the countersigned divorce decree that should be waiting there for him. He had that one last thread to cut before he was free of Shelly.

"What's wrong," Heather asked after an uncomfortable silence.

"I like you," he said, deciding not to pussyfoot around the thing, but just put his feelings on the line and accept rejection if it came. He was a writer after all, and he should be used to rejection by now. "I like you a lot, and I'd like to get to know you better when this is over."

Heather raised an eyebrow. "When this is over?"

"When my divorce is final."

She watched him, silent now, her face impassive, her feelings a mystery.

Jim continued, nervous. "I understand if you don't feel the same way. I just don't have the heart for games, and I don't want you to think I'm playing them with you."

Heather continued to give him the thousand-yard stare, her arms folded on the table, leaning toward him.

"You're married." She blinked, then and examined her fingernails. "Do you love her?"

He shrugged. "Maybe. I know I did in the beginning, but we don't even like each other anymore, so any love still between us is poisoned."

"What happened? What made you fall out of *like*?"

That, Jim thought, *is simple.*

"I didn't pay enough attention to her. She writes for the paper in Boston, but at the end of the day she puts her job away, and I never could. I am what I do, twenty-four/seven."

Heather nodded as if to say, *yeah, yeah, what else.*

"We've been together for three years, married for two. She started cheating after the first year. I found out about her first affair and got into a fight with the guy. Ended up in jail.

"I got out the next day and told her I forgave her. Shelly said it was very noble of me, but that she didn't forgive me. After that she didn't try to hide it."

"Did you ever hit her?"

"No. Never."

Heather leaned back in her chair and watched him for a few moments, then said, "I believe you."

Jim sighed, but did not relax completely. He was still hanging by a thread.

"There are things about me you don't know," she said. "Some of them are not good things, and I can't tell you about them yet. Maybe later, but not now. Can you accept that?"

"Yes," Jim said.

"You say that you want to get to know me, but I'll give you a chance to back out now." She was shaking, Jim noticed. As if trying to hold back some pent-up force within. "If you were smart you'd take it. I wouldn't fault you for getting away now."

Jim said nothing.

"Someday I'll have to tell you things about myself, if we last that long. It will complicate your life more than you know. Do you still want to get to know me?"

"Yes," Jim said. "I do."

Heather reached across the table, pulled him forward, and kissed him. With an aggression that both startled and excited him, Heather pulled him from his chair, across the room to her bed.

Finally, she released him from the kiss and pushed him onto the narrow, squeaky mattress.

"I like you too," she said with a smile. "A lot."

Bill enjoyed a quick dip in the cold water, but grew bored. Michael seemed to have come down from whatever high he was on and sat on the granite slab, feet dangling in the water. Every now and then he would toss a rock in the lake and study the rings it made on the water.

Camp was fully focused on Tracy's tits, and was not shy about the attention he paid them. Tracy, for her part, didn't seem to mind. She'd gone into the water in a pair of Daisy Duke cutoffs and a T-shirt, and had since shed the shirt.

Bill really couldn't blame Camp. Her tits were quite nice.

"Hey guys, I think I'll head back up," Michael said. He grimaced, clutching his stomach as he rose.

"What's wrong?" Bill asked.

"Breakfast isn't sitting well," he said. "I'll be fine. Think I'll take a nap though."

Bill nodded. "See you later then."

Michael did a slow march around the lake, then disappeared up the trail to the lodge.

Burned out, Bill thought. *Too much excitement.*

He turned back to the sound of splashing water, and found Camp and Tracy wrapped around each other, bobbing up and down in the water.

Feeling like a third wheel, Bill rose and headed toward the trail back to the lodge.

"I'll see you crazy kids later," he said. "Don't forget to come up for air."

Camp, looking like he was trying very hard to pull Tracy's tongue out with his teeth, waved him away.

Bill found the lodge empty, and decided now was a good time to take another swipe at the creative block that had been pissing him off for the past few weeks.

CHAPTER 12

The First Cut

Morning slipped quietly into afternoon, and Jim stepped into the light again, combing his hair back with his fingers as Heather followed him outside and closed her cabin door. Clouds overhead threw shade over the fire ring, where Ryan, Susan, and Casper sat.

"We're going to catch hell," Jim said, but he smiled. He didn't really care.

Heather said nothing, but grabbed his hand and pulled him forward. "Mind if we join you?"

The others turned to them, and Jim clearly saw Ryan's face break into a grin.

Susan looked almost shocked.

Casper gave them a sleepy once over and nodded before turning back to his conversation with Susan.

Ryan rose and met them half way. "Heather, do you have a minute?"

"Is it time for our talk?" she asked, and gave Jim's hand a squeeze before letting it go.

Jim, loathe to let her out of his sight even in for a

moment, said, "Don't believe a thing he says about me," and moved on to the fire ring.

Susan met him with a smile. "So, are you having fun?"

"Yes," Jim said. "Thanks for inviting me."

"Rich was much better at organizing these get-togethers than I."

"Frankly," Casper said, turning his lazy gaze toward her, "I'm enjoying the more relaxed pace. Richard would have had our every waking moment planned for us in advanced."

Casper turned to Jim. "He was a wonderful fellow, but he kept a very rigid schedule."

"How was Richard involved in the genre?" Jim asked, suddenly curious about the Hacks founder.

"May I?" Casper asked Susan, and when she gave a nod he turned back to Jim. "Richard Bonkowski was, in his early days, responsible for the resurgence of fantasy and horror beyond the few big names of the seventies and eighties. He was an editor for Hammer House, and by the time it was swallowed up by one of the big six, he was half owner. After that he started a chain of bookstores in California." Casper gave Susan one of his rare smiles. "That was where he met this lovely young lady."

Susan laughed.

"You flatterer," then to Jim, "Rich was forty when we married. I was … younger."

Jim had thought as much. Susan looked thirty-something now, too young to be a rich widow.

"I managed his store in San Francisco. He came in one day, just browsing, and asked me where I kept the John McDonalds. I helped him, and that was it. I didn't know who he was. He came back the next day and asked me what new authors I recommend, then asked me on a date. He'd taken me out three times before I found out he was my boss."

Casper laughed. "I love that story. Very romantic."

Susan's smile faded then. "Rich had a heart attack last year, a few weeks after Hacks. You were short-listed last year too. I wish he'd had a chance to meet you. He really liked your work."

That reminded Jim of something he'd forgotten about. "In my letter you said I was an alternate, but that one of your planned guests had an unfortunate accident."

Susan frowned.

"Yes," she said. "I won't name names, but the *gentleman* is a screen writer. You probably know who he is."

Jim thought, but shook his head.

"The man *accidentally* had sex with a fourteen-year-old girl," Casper said. He shook his head. "Writers are a strange lot. I suspect we all belong in prisons or asylums."

"Son-of-a-bitch!"

They turned as one and found Bill standing beside Camp's Mustang, hands on his hips. "Camp is going to kill somebody!"

Bill put pen to paper in the comfortable old rocking chair in the lodge's large main room, pleased to see the writer's block had gone. Packed its bags while he was looking the other way and vacated the premises.

In its place was a tidal wave of coherent thought and beautiful words. Stable nouns, a few self-important pronouns that always managed to sneak in, tense verbs, ready to spring from the page and bitch-slap his readers. Action and thought in symbiosis.

Bill loved his job!

When the creative rush had played itself out, he had seven fresh pages. Good pages. There would be more later, as always. Again he had confronted The Block, and again had kicked its ass.

He rose finally, ripping the pages from the notebook, folding them, and putting them in his pocket. Two hours had bled away while he worked. He decided to reward himself before joining the party again.

He found Ryan and Heather on the patio, deep in what sounded suspiciously like negotiations, and passed without interrupting them. Susan, Jim, and Casper were sitting at the fire ring.

He'd have to be quick.

The remaining Smirnoffs in Camp's cooler would be warm by now, the ice having melted, but a warm drink was better than no drink at all.

Maybe I'll take a walk to the lake, let them chill in the water.

A fine plan, he decided. Camp and Tracy *should* be finished by now.

Better grab three then. Tracy might want one.

Hide them under his shirt and sneak behind the cabins to the lake trail, and when he was done, drop the empty bottles down the shithouse.

Bill noticed something wrong with the Mustang the moment he saw it. The way it sat tilted to one side. He stooped, looked closer, and saw that both tires on the driver's side were flat.

"Son-of-a-bitch! Camp is going to kill somebody!"

He crouched, inspecting the front tire. There was a two-inch-long slash along the sidewall.

One guess who did this, kids!

He rose and crossed to the other side of the Mustang.

"What's wrong?"

It was Ryan, Heather running at his side. The others were close behind. He ignored them for the moment while he inspected the passenger side tires. The front was flat, also slashed, but the rear was fully inflated.

As if the slasher had been interrupted before he could finish.

Bill scanned the trees, cupping hands over his eyes to block out fingers of sunlight that broke through gathering clouds.

No Yohan. No anyone.

"Shit."

Bill turned and found Ryan checking out the damage. He seemed almost to deflate before Bill's eyes.

"That crazy fucker." This came out in a croak, as if through a parched throat. Ryan was very pale.

Then the others were there.

"What is it?" Susan was trying to shoulder her way between Jim and Ryan. "What happened?"

"Someone slashed the tires," Ryan said.

"He came back," Susan said. "God damn it, he came back."

"He might still be here," Bill said, his voice low enough that only Jim, Ryan, and Susan heard. "Ryan, go check the lodge out. Lock the back door and make sure he's not in there. Then come back and let us know if it's clear."

Ryan nodded and sprinted away.

"Susan, wait for Ryan, then get into the lodge and lock it up."

Bill turned to Jim. "Camp and Tracy are at the lake. Tell Camp what's going on and get them up here."

Then Bill turned and strode away, fists swinging at his side. "I'm going to look for Yahoo."

Ryan breezed through the main room. There was no place to hide there, and a quick search satisfied him it was safe. Slowing down in the hallway that led to the back entrance, he tensed, expecting Yohan to spring from the kitchen door like a giant knife wielding Jack-In-The-Box.

It did not happen, and Ryan relaxed a little when he found the kitchen empty. The utility room at the end of the hallway, also empty.

The back door was open, and Ryan tried to remember if it had been earlier. He wasn't sure, but he didn't think so. Ryan closed and locked the door, then moved into the front room, taking the stairs to the second floor.

The second floor was a loft converted into three rooms. The stairs came up in the middle room, which was bare. No furniture, no knife-wielding maniacs either. Susan's room was through the door to the right, his to the left. He checked Susan's first. Clear.

Ryan's room was as he had left it. His tackle box sat beside the bed. He opened it and grabbed the hatchet and his knife. He pocketed the knife and slipped the leather hood from the hatchet's blade.

Feeling a little braver with his hatchet in hand, Ryan went back downstairs.

Jim felt vulnerable, alone on the trail with that bastard Yohan still unaccounted for. Maybe close by, maybe not.

Just keep moving, he thought. *Moving targets are harder to kill.*

He knew he was making too much of it, the man was certainly an asshole, a peeping Tom, and now a vandal, but that didn't make him a killer.

Jim still felt safer moving. He didn't care to test that assumption, logical or not.

Winded by the time he reached the outhouse, he let himself stop for just a moment to catch his breath, and scan the lake. He couldn't see Camp or Tracy yet.

Jim moved on.

He rounded the lake, the granite slab at the far end coming into view. Tracy lay naked on it, sunning herself. The stone was wet around her, dark with lake water.

But it didn't look like water. It was too dark, and she was too still.

He slowed as he drew nearer, not wanting to be there. Not wanting to see her. Not wanting his morbid suspicions confirmed.

Want or not, he went to her, and there was no doubt.

Not water, but blood.

Too still because she was dead.

But he had to be certain. Fighting the impulse to turn tail and run, Jim crouched down.

The dark hair covering the back of her head, parting around her neck and laying against the bloody stone, looked messed, and there was a small patch missing. Torn out. Her head was misshapen.

Jim braced himself and put a hand on her shoulder. Her skin was cold, but that could have been because of the lake water. Slowly, he rolled Tracy onto her back.

Most of her face was gone, her nose pushed inside her head, the skin from forehead to chin shredded like hamburger, her mouth a shapeless, toothless hole.

Tracy still had her eyes though. They stared up at him, wide, lidless, glaring in eternal shock.

Jim dropped her and stumbled, falling hard on his ass. He was up and running before he felt the pain.

Running faster than he ever had before. Like the devil was close behind him, his pitchfork already halfway up his ass.

Bill felt as if the woods had swallowed him up.

The Devil's Tail Road had been intimidating even in the relative security of Yohan's Jeep. On foot it was fucking eerie.

How far had he walked? How many twists and turns?

Bill had no idea, but he did know one thing, none of them had felt the need to hike it. They had all arrived with four wheels under them. But there were footprints, every so often. Boot prints. Cowboy boots. Coming and going.

Those boot prints were the only sign he found of Yohan. Then he found the Jeep, tucked snug between two huge trees beside the road. Yohan hadn't even bothered hiding it.

Maybe Yahoo The Swedish Meatball hadn't planned on anyone coming this far to look for him.

Maybe he left the keys in it.

Bill doubted it. Things were never that easy.

The doors were unlocked, but he didn't find the keys.

Wishing Camp were there, he backed out and slammed the door shut. Keys wouldn't have been an issue for Camp. He'd have had it hot-wired in under a minute.

There was no point walking any further. If the Jeep was still parked here, then Yohan was still somewhere between it and the lodge.

Bill considered letting the air out of the Jeeps tires, but knew it was a bad idea. Instead, he reached into the driver's side door and released the back hatch. He searched and found a spare tire, but no jack or tire iron. He figured the spare would be flat, but when he pulled it out and let it drop on the hard-packed dirt of the forest floor, it bounced.

Bill walked back down The Devil's Tail, rolling the spare tire ahead of him. Hoping like hell it would fit Camp's Mustang.

He made his slow progression back to the lodge with the uncanny, the *unsettling,* feeling of being watched.

SHOCKLINES

From: Matt Schwartz
To: warehouse@shocklines.com
Subject: Hacks Club Author's Books

Please secure ASAP any copies you can find of limited and hardcover editions written by the following authors involved in the Hacks Club Massacre. Do not list these books for sale on shocklines.com. Please remove any copies of these books already listed from the catalog and hold them.

Bill Koch, Jeff Campbell, Tracy West, Jim Eldridge, Michael Smith, and H Casper.

Also, hold any rare editions published by Ryan Stahl's Delirium Books.

I've secured limited edition rights for Heather Woods's

Unstable, and will print a limited run (750 to 1,000 copies) by the end of the year.

Once Unstable is printed, I will hold an auction to sell the entire lot. All profits will go to a fund set up to benefit surviving family members of the Hack's Club Massacre victims.

These books are now highly prized by collectors, so make this your top priority.

All the best,
  Matt

CHAPTER 13

The Killer or The Hack

Jim didn't remember his panicked flight from the lake, only moments, terror-stricken flashes from an over-imaginative mind playing tricks on him. A grunt behind him, a clawed hand swiping at him from the trees as he broke from the trail into the clearing, a bloodstained knife finding his back as he pounded the locked front door of the lodge. Faces pressed against the windows while he slid bleeding to the porch.

And then he was inside, hands closing over his arms, leading him forcibly to the closest chair. Voices babbled barely decipherable words, muffled by the pounding in his head. But their meaning was clear.

What the hell happened?

"Tracy's dead," he managed between sucking great gasps of air. "Can't find Camp."

Silent, blanched faces stared at him. For a while no one spoke. Then Ryan stepped forward. "How?"

"Killed … by the lake," Jim said, and speaking the

words gave it more weight. For a moment he thought he might faint. "Someone smashed her head on the rocks."

He felt the world shift before him, but a sudden pain in his shoulder, Ryan squeezing it, strong nails digging at flesh, brought it back into focus.

Behind the others, Heather said, "Oh, no," and began to sway on her feet. Her eyes rolled to the whites and she said a name before crumpling to the floor.

Dave.

Susan and Casper lifted her between them, and placed her gently on the couch.

"Who the hell is Dave?" Ryan said, turning back to Jim.

Jim looked past Ryan, toward Heather, slowly fighting her way back to consciousness.

He's watching, she had said the night before.

He's going to be mad.

"Jim?" Ryan said.

"I don't know."

"Guys," a shaking voice behind them. For a moment Jim thought Heather was talking in her sleep again. But Susan stepped forward. "Where is Michael?"

"Shit," Ryan shouted. He'd forgotten completely about Michael, and could have kicked himself for it. "Last time I saw him, he was headed to the lake with Camp and Tracy."

The chilling reality of the situation began to settle over Ryan.

Tracy was dead.

Camp and Michael were unaccounted for.

Bill was alone, somewhere on The Devil's Tail.

Out there, somewhere, a killer waited.

"Camp was swimming," he said. "Did you see his clothes anywhere?"

"No." Comprehension dawned on Jim's face. "Camp's gun!"

"If you didn't see it down there, we have to assume Yohan has it now."

Casper, sitting next to Heather, cradling her, cleared his throat. "Perhaps we should call the authorities. There is a radio, right?"

Susan nodded and started down the hallway.

Ryan grabbed Jim's arm, and pulled him to his feet. "We need to check the cabins, make sure Camp and Michael aren't in one of them." He slapped the handle of his hatchet into Jim's hand.

Jim nodded, wrapped his fingers in a death grip around its handle, and followed him to the door.

"Casper, can you stay with Heather and Susan?"

Casper nodded, then rocked the whimpering woman in his arms.

"Thanks," Ryan said. "We'll be right back."

They stayed together, searching side by side, Jim with the hatchet and Ryan with the longest blade of his Boy Scout Knife leading the way.

At each cabin, Ryan's terror peaked, and each door he opened made him feel like Pandora, opening not just one, but half a dozen evil boxes.

Other analogies occurred to him as he faced each cabin in turn; the Killer or the Hack, the Psycho shower scene, Stephen King's Body Under The Blanket. He wished he could still the disturbing chatter in his head.

After the surge of terror each closed cabin door inspired, there was an anticlimactic fizzle. Not relief. He knew each empty cabin was only a momentary reprieve, stringing him along to the next.

By the time they'd reached the last cabin, Jim's cabin, he almost hoped a knife-wielding Yohan would pop out at him.

Any hope that they'd find Camp or Michael had died.

Again, nothing.

They sprinted back to the lodge, Susan gasped when they threw the door open, and slammed it shut.

"They aren't in the cabins," Jim said. Then to Susan, "Sorry, didn't mean to scare you."

"It's okay," Susan said.

"Did you get hold of anyone?" Ryan asked.

"No," Susan said. "The radio is dead."

"Dead?" Panic gnawed at his nerves.

Beside him, Jim groaned.

Susan dropped onto the couch next to Heather. "The battery is gone," she said. "It's a 12 volt, and I can't find a spare."

Heather, still in her uneasy sleep, spoke again. "He's coming."

Minutes later Jim was back outside, shaking as he accompanied Ryan down The Devil's Tail Road, trying to block the image of Tracy's ruined face from his mind.

Bill had vanished down this evergreen cave a half hour earlier and not yet returned.

Jim clutched the hatchet, his arm tensed, aching. He hoped if he had to use it, he could be quick and accurate.

Ryan had left his knife with Susan, and carried the axe they'd fetched from the wood stack with both hands. He looked very comfortable with it, and Jim took some solace in that.

Through the occasional opening in their evergreen canopy, Jim saw thickening clouds, bloated and gray. The violet of a setting sun lined them. Twilight had crept upon them. Soon the dark would come.

The sound of a gunshot set fire to his already fried nerves.

The gunshot was close. Bill let go of the rolling tire and fell to his knees, facing the woods. Instinctively making himself a smaller target as he scanned the trees for the shooter.

Something crashed through the trees, stomping underbrush and dead wood. The woods were darker now though, and he saw nothing but shadows beyond the trees.

"Watch out!"

Bill recognized Jim's voice. A second later there was another shout and the sound of a body hitting the dirt.

Jim followed Ryan down The Devil's Tail. Running toward the sound of the gunshot against his better judgment.

They rounded one of the many sharp bends, and Jim saw something black and round, rolling very fast at them.

"Watch out!"

But Ryan was moving too fast, was too focused on the woods, and he met it at full speed.

It took his legs out from under him, flipping him into the air. The axe flew from his hand, and he landed hard, sprawled out on the hard-packed dirt and stone with a winded grunt.

A moment later Bill came into view, eyes wide. Amped. He picked up Ryan's axe as he crouched beside him.

Ryan did not move.

Jim slid to a stop, tripped over a jut of rock, and fell to his knees. The pain was instant and intense. Whiteout pain, like a flare in his brain. When it faded, Jim found himself face first in the dirt.

"I hope to fuck you can still walk," Bill said, yanking Jim off the ground by the back of his shirt.

Ryan stood next to them, blood and dust caked on his face, his nose smashed against his cheek and eyes swelling, the cut on his head opened again.

"Fug," he said, cupping his smashed nose. *Fuck.* "Ged ub, ledgo!" *Get up, let's go!*

Jim stood with Bill's help, wobbled, his knees not screaming pain anymore, but still throbbing mightily. "Tracy's dead."

Bill froze for a moment, then his face whipped back toward Jim. "Dead?"

"Murgerg," Ryan said. *Murdered.*

Bill grabbed Jim by his collar and pulled him closer. "Camp?"

"I don't know. I couldn't find him or Michael." Jim half expected Bill to explode, to throttle him. He braced himself for a trip back to the dirt.

It didn't happen. Bill released him.

"We should go," Jim said.

Bill nodded. "Yes." He handed the axe back to Ryan, then bent and righted the tire again.

Ryan gave the tire a hateful look, then said, "Doodidi-da." *Good idea.*

"We'll have to come back for another if we want to get out of here without busting an axle," Bill said. "If this one even fits."

He started rolling the tire again, not running, but making a good pace. Jim and Ryan followed, limping like a pair of cripples.

"Has Susan radioed out yet?"

"Radio's dead," Jim said. "Yohan stole the battery."

Bill grunted out a sound of pure disgust. "If I get my hands on that fucker, he's going to take a fast trip to the bottom of the canyon."

Jim believed him, and if that happy moment came, he vowed that he'd be there to help give Yohan a proper send off.

Heather sat near the fireplace, more for the fire's light than for heat. Every gas light in the main room burned, but they were not enough. The Dark had come, and Heather didn't think there would be enough light in the world to shield them against it.

Susan left Casper on the sofa, silent and looking more

angry than scared, pacing back and forth from the couch to Heather's chair. Every few minutes she would say, "They should be back any minute now, you'll see," or "we're okay, we'll be fine."

Heather didn't think she believed it.

When they heard the gunshot, Susan went silent. Soon after, the nervous pacing stopped, and she sat down next to Casper.

When she began to weep, Heather left her seat next to the fire and sat next to her. Casper took them both in his large arms and held them.

Heather did not believe Jim, Ryan, or Bill would come back. Nor Camp and Michael. All they could do now was wait out the night and hope Yohan would not come back for them.

It was a feeble hope, and the tighter she held it, the weaker it seemed.

The stomping of feet on the porch made Heather and Susan scream. Casper jumped to his feet, held the carving knife before him as he approached the door.

Then she heard Jim's voice, and her terror became sobbing relief. She ran for the door, reached it just ahead of Casper, and fumbled with the lock.

"Let me," Casper said, and pushed her shaking hand aside.

Jim, Ryan, and Bill rushed in and slammed the door shut behind them. Ryan engaged the lock on the knob, then, grabbing the chair from next to the fireplace, braced the door with it.

Bill picked a spot in front of the window, and stood staring into the dark. His expression was fierce. He looked tired, but unharmed. Jim limped to Heather's side and put his arms around her. "Doing okay?"

She nodded, but did not speak. She buried her face in his chest, locked her hands behind his back, vowing not to let him leave her side again. She thought she'd lost him, and it hurt more than she could have imagined.

"Oh my!" Susan said through fresh tears. "Ryan!"

Jim broke Heather's grip. "Where's the first aid kit?"

"I'll get it," Susan said, and hurried into the kitchen.

Jim followed her.

"Damnit, Ryan. What happened to you?" Casper asked.

Ryan's face was a mess of blood and dirt, his nose bent grotesquely to one side. What wasn't covered in blood and filth was very pale. He'd obviously lost a lot of blood.

"Sit," Casper said, pointing at the couch.

Ryan nodded and sat down, slumped against the arm and tipping his head back.

Next to him, examining the damage, Casper said, "We can fix this. I need two rags and some water."

Still in front of the window, Bill crossed his arms over his chest.

"I'll get them," Heather said. She stood, and on her way to the kitchen, she met Susan and Jim. Jim stayed with her, carrying a water-filled bowl for her on their way back.

With the first aid kit open on the couch beside Casper, Jim held the bowl while Casper cleaned Ryan's face with a wet rag.

Ryan's breathing quickened when Casper wiped around his nose, but he didn't scream. Once cleaned, the damage didn't seem as bad. The cut on his forehead trickled blood, but there were no cuts on his face, just a roadmap of scratches, and the flattened nose.

"This is going to hurt," Casper said.

Ryan nodded, closed his eyes.

Grabbing Ryan's nose between his thumb and forefinger, Casper wrenched it straight. It crunched like a broken twig.

Ryan screamed, but only once, and when Casper lowered his hand, Ryan's nose was on straight again. Bleeding freely, but no longer looking like something squashed and spackled to his face with blood and dirt.

"Thanks," Ryan said, touching his nose gingerly.

"We're not finished yet." Casper plucked a roll of medical tape from the first aid kit and pulled a strip loose.

"Looking good," Bill said. He'd given up his watch and joined the group around Casper and Ryan. "You were a medic, right."

"Yes," Casper said, laying the first strip carefully over the bridge of Ryan's nose, then across his cheeks. "Vietnam."

"Too bad you don't have your sixteen with you."

Casper grunted his response and put another strip of tape over Ryan's nose.

"Did you find Michael or Camp?" Susan seemed to have composed herself again. Heather saw the look she gave Ryan, a mixture of relief and unblinking tenderness.

I'm not the only one then, she thought, and for some reason she couldn't explain to herself, the thought comforted her. She took Jim's hand and held it tight.

"No," Jim said.

"That shot," Bill said. "I'd bet my next royalty check

that was his gun. Either he's still out there, or Yohan has it."

"Are you sure it's Yohan?" Heather asked, and received half a dozen surprised looks.

"Who else?" Bill asked.

"Dave," Jim said.

Heather looked away.

"Who's Dave?"

It was time, she decided. Even if it was only a paranoid suspicion, they had to know.

Everything.

Heather tightened her grip on Jim's hand, unwilling to let that comfort go. Even if what she was about to confess drove him away, she would have the comfort of his hand in hers while she talked about things she had once thought behind her forever.

"Dave is my husband," Heather said.

Every face turned to her, each one shocked. Even Casper paused his work to regard her.

Jim's most of all, and though he didn't try to pull away from her, she could read the hurt on his face.

Heather sighed, paused, and began her story, "I'm not who you think I am."

CHAPTER 14

Heather's Story

"Heather Woods was my best friend when I was a little girl," she began. "She died of leukemia when I was six." Heather, or whoever she really was, smiled. A sad smile that died quickly.

"My name," she paused, "my *old* name was Betty Conway. When I was sixteen I met Dave Randal. He was twenty-one, and my mother hated him, but I wouldn't stop seeing him."

She watched her feet while she spoke. Her grip on Jim's hand remained tight.

"My father was gone by then, I never found out where. I was pregnant before I turned seventeen, and when it started to show, my mother found out and told me to leave. So I married Dave, and he moved me as far away from what was left of my family as he could afford."

Outside a cougar screamed. It sounded uncannily like a shrieking woman. The sound brought startled gasps. Bill's face turned once again toward the window.

Heather seemed not to have noticed.

"I never saw much of the new town we moved to. He had a house waiting for us when we arrived, his uncle's he said. Our first night there was the first time he hit me." Her face showed no emotion, but tears welled in her eyes. "We hadn't even fought, and he wasn't mad about anything. He held me against a wall and punched me in the stomach. Three times, like it was the most natural thing in the world to do.

"I lost my baby," she said. "A girl. I was going to name her Lily. I slept in the bathtub that night. He barred the door to keep me inside. I slept with Lily on my chest. The next day he came in with a garbage bag and told me to throw it away before it started stinking. I put Lily in the bag, and he left. I tried to get out, but he locked me in again.

"I heard him in the yard behind the house and slid the window open." Her neutral expression changed to pure loathing. "He was barbecuing in the back yard with his uncle. Cooking hotdogs, drinking beer. They sat in lawn chairs and watched his uncle's dog ripping open the garbage bag. They laughed while it ate Lily, like it was doing tricks or playing with a toy."

She winced as Jim's hand clenched on hers. His face was red. "Sorry," he said, and loosened his grip. He did not let go, though, and Heather's other hand closed over it.

"He came back that night like nothing was wrong. He explained to me that it was for the best. We weren't ready for kids. He didn't even like them. I went crazy when he said that. I screamed, I punched him, I even bit him. It must have been the sight of his blood that set him off that time, because he gave me the worst beating I have ever had. He beat me to the floor, and he kept on beating me until I thought I would die.

"I woke up in the basement. He'd painted the windows black and torn out the staircase. There was a ladder leading up to the basement door. I was handcuffed to a bed, naked." She blushed at the memory, the shame still fresh in her mind.

In a low, sneering voice, she said, *"If you're going to behave like a wild animal I'll treat you like one."*

Her knees wobbled beneath her, and if Jim hadn't been holding her, she would have fallen. Jim and Casper helped her to the couch and sat her next to Ryan, who put an arm over her shoulder, gave a little squeeze of a hug, and released her. Then Jim was next to her again, and she leaned into him.

"He raped me, then left me down there. He pulled the ladder up after him, so even after he finally took the handcuffs off, I wouldn't be able to get out. He kept me down there for five years."

"Why," Susan asked, her face gray, sickly.

"Because he was a sick, twisted son of a bitch. He brought his uncle and a few of his cousins down to show me off. They took turns with me. Sometimes he'd bring them over and they'd all have me at the same time, they raped me with anything they could get their hands on. Flashlights, beer bottles, and ..."

Heather released Jim's hand, buried her face in both of hers and sobbed.

"Jesus," Susan said, "Maybe you should lie down for a while."

"No. I need to get it out."

Jim grabbed Heather's hand, and gave it a gentle squeeze.

"He never left me alone. Ever. But one night he didn't come down. And he didn't show up the next night, either. I pulled the mattress off the bed and leaned the frame against the wall, beneath one of the windows. Then I wrapped the bed sheets around my forearm and used the wooden slats like ladder rungs and climbed to the top of the bed frame. The window was small and I didn't know if I could even fit through, but I had to try. I busted out as much glass as I could. It was a tight fit, but I finally was able to squeeze my way through. And just like that, I was free. I ran and I never looked back.

"I made my way back home, but Mama was gone. So I used Heather's name to check into a battered woman's shelter. Before I knew it, I'd built a new life. That was eight years ago.

"A few days after my Hacks invitation arrived, I got a letter from Dave. No return address, just his name. Dave. *I know who you are.* So I left, stayed in hotels, and then came here. I never thought he could find me here."

"What were you planning to do after this week?" Jim asked.

"I don't know."

Jim wrapped his arms around her. "So, now that you've told me, what do I call you, Heather or Betty?"

"Don't call me Betty," she said. "I don't ever want to be Betty again."

"It can't be him," Jim said, trying to sound reasonable,

calm. Trying to convince himself while he convinced Heather. "There's no way he could track you here."

"That's not true," Bill said.

Jim shot him a *shut up* look, and Bill returned it with a *make me* look.

"Not trying to piss on your parade, Jim. Just saying it straight. We can't afford the luxury of bullshit right now." Then to Heather, "Did you use aliases to travel?"

She shook her head. "No, my license, social security number, credit cards, all issued to Heather Woods."

"And your flight," Bill said. "Dave could have tracked you to Lewiston, Idaho. From there to here though ...," he let his words drift, then turned to Susan. "How many people know we're here?"

"Yohan, a few Department of Lands people, and the driver who picked you up from the airport."

Bill nodded, seemed to consider, then spoke. "It's not likely. Even if he tracked you to Lewiston, he'd have to be a damn good detective to track you here."

Heather looked unconvinced.

"He's right," Jim said. "We may have to deal with Dave soon enough, but he's not here."

"Someone's coming," Casper said. He grabbed his knife from the arm of the chair and stood.

Jim turned to the window, saw a streak of man-shaped darkness dart past the window, and heard footfalls on the porch. Then the door knob rattled.

"Are you fucks going to let me in or what?" Camp's voice came from the other side of the door. "There's a fucking psycho out here!"

Bill suddenly felt much better about their chances. They had Camp, not to mention his gun, back on their side.

"Frankenhand is the only reason Yahoo isn't dead," Camp said, looking disgusted with himself. "I think I winged him though."

"What happened?" Susan came into the room with Ryan, a mug of coffee in hand for Camp, who'd complained that his caffeine level was too low.

"We were swimming. I had to take a shit. When I went back I found Yahoo standing over Tracy. He saw me before I could draw, and I've been tracking him through the woods since." Camp ran a hand through his tangled hair. "Lost my favorite hat too."

Camp took an offered mug of coffee from Susan and drained most of it in one swallow.

"I was lost for a while. It was dark when I finally found him hiding under a deadfall. Like I said, I think I winged him. He fell, anyway. Then he disappeared." He pointed at Bill. "If you guys hadn't made such a racket on the road I'd probably still be lost out there."

"Did you see Michael anywhere?" Ryan asked. His nose was swelling beneath the tape, his voice was thick and nasal.

Camp shook his head. Downing the last of his coffee. "Last I saw Michael, he was leaving the lake. What were you guys doing anyway?"

Bill had been watching Heather, and was marginally pleased that the reality of their situation was sinking in. Camp had fingered Yohan, and that let her psycho husband off the hook. Things were still bad, but at least now she knew it wasn't her fault.

"We were looking for him," Jim said, nodding toward Bill.

"I found Yohan's Jeep down the road," Bill said. "Yohan slashed a couple of your tires, so I stole his spare. We need to go back for one more. Or, you could hot-wire his Jeep."

Camp seemed to consider that, looked around the room and shook his head. "Jeep's not big enough for all of us, but we can bring it back and take a tire. The Mustang will be tight, but we'll all fit."

Bill thought Camp might say something like that. He wouldn't want to leave his Mustang.

"Let's make sure his tires fit first," Bill said.

"You'd think," Jim said, "that someone who makes his living as a wilderness guide would carry a gun."

"Yes," Ryan said. "I was wondering about that."

"No," Susan said. "He told me he's not allowed to carry or own firearms."

All faces turned to her.

"Ex-con?" Camp asked.

Susan nodded. "Almost killed a man in a bar fight when he was younger. Spent a few years in prison because of it."

Bill looked at her, incredulous. "You hired an ex-con to keep us safe up here?"

Casper, who'd been sitting quietly, turned to Bill.

"No need to beat up on her," he said, wincing as he stood. He took a stiff-legged step between Bill and Susan. "I know at least one of us has spent some time in jail."

He looked pointedly at Bill.

Bill saw himself stepping forward and laying Casper out cold, but held back.

It wasn't the time.

"You and Ryan stay here," Bill said, glaring at Casper. He picked up Ryan's axe and walked to the door. "Camp, Jim, let's go. Shouldn't take too long to get another tire. Then we're outa here."

Casper raised an eyebrow. "And who put you in charge of this disaster?"

"I did," Bill said. "Live with it or start walking."

Bill swung the door open and stepped out into the porch, waiting. Camp followed him out, gun drawn.

Heather stopped Jim before he could join them.

"Be careful," she said, then kissed him.

"I will," Jim said, then stepped out and closed the door between them.

Heather went to the small window at the far end of the room and stared out. She could see them, Bill jacking up the Mustang while Jim and Camp stood guard. Bill changed two of the flats using Camp's and Yohan's spares. When they finished, the Mustang leaned to one side, like a dog lifting its leg to piss on a tree.

Bill opened the trunk and pulled out a flashlight, then two bottles from a cooler inside. He tested the light, handed one of the bottles to Jim, then they were off.

She watched until they were out of sight, then sighed and rejoined the others.

Casper had gone silent again. Not just looking pissed this time, but actually pissed. A bit of her respect for him faded at the sight of his plump, sneering face.

She wanted to yell at him to stop it. At least *someone* had taken charge. Instead she walked to the fire and stood next to Susan and Ryan. Neither spoke, but their presence was comforting.

She felt so stupid, spilling her guts to a roomful of strangers. She knew how unlikely it was that Dave would find her here, it was why she'd come, but a small part of her still believed he was out there somewhere, a silent figure stalking the night.

Who knows, maybe that crazy guide is working for Dave too.

That could not be the case though. Those kinds of unlikely alliances only happened in fiction.

Still, the thought would not die so easily.

Heavy feet stomped up the steps, shattered the tense silence.

They turned as one toward the door.

"It's him," Susan whispered, her barely audible voice shaking.

Ryan braced himself against the fireplace mantle and pulled a fireplace poker from the rack on the wall. Holding it like a bat, he approached the door in slow steps.

Casper did the same, the carving knife in his shaking right hand.

The locked door knob rattled.

A step closer to the door, Ryan raised the poker over his head.

Casper wrapped his other hand over the knife's handle, steadying the blade, and took another slow step forward. He looked like a large, elderly knight, with a ridiculously short sword.

Something pounded the door, shaking it in his frame. The chair bracing the door made ominous cracking sounds.

Heather and Susan screamed.

Ryan and Casper stopped in their tracks.

For a moment there was nothing.

Then the door smashed inward. The fractured chair skidded forward and the door slammed the floor in two pieces.

He stood framed in the door, a monstrous silhouette framed by a deep blue night, regarding them in turn.

Then he stepped inside.

Ryan stood frozen in place.

Casper cried out and dropped the knife, clutching his chest. He fell to his knees, pale and sweating as the man stepped toward him.

The killing blow fell, and Casper raised an arm to block it. The blade, large and rusty, hacked through Casper's arm, through the top of his head, through his neck, and into his chest.

Screaming, Ryan rushed forward and brought the poker down against the killer's head with a crack.

The man let out a small grunt, then yanked the blade free of Casper and turned to face Ryan. The blade came down again in a wide, swishing arch.

Ryan brought the poker up and steel met iron, throwing sparks. The impact slammed Ryan against the wall. His head struck wood with a crack, and he sagged to the floor.

Screaming, Heather and Susan ran for the back door.

Something echoed through the night, a howl or a scream. Maybe in the canyon below the lodge, maybe closer.

Jim paused. "Guys, you hear that?"

"Probably a cougar down in the canyon," Camp said. "C'mon, lets move."

Jim hurried to catch up, then slowed to their easy pace.

"Not too far now," Bill said. "I think."

But the road went on and on. Short straights broken by sharp twists. Once they heard something crash through the trees to their left, but when Bill turned his light toward the sound they found nothing. It could have been Yohan, or Heather's crazy stalker husband, or Alan Funt getting ready to jump out and yell *surprise, you're on Candid-fucking-Camera*!

It occurred to Jim for the first time, that the whole thing might be some kind of a scam, like the phony who-done-it setups you'd find at mystery lover's conventions. Maybe Susan, Ryan and Casper were playing some kind of crazy Hacks prank on the rest of them, and the person who cracked the case got to come back again next year.

But he knew it wasn't the case. Tracy's shattered skull and ruined face was the real thing.

"There," Bill said as a faint disc of light fell over the dusty white surface of Yohan's Jeep.

"I bet if we search we'll find a gun hidden in there somewhere," Jim said. "Yohan doesn't strike me as the kind of man who plays by the rules."

"No," Camp said. "If he had a gun he wouldn't leave it in there. He'd have it with him, and he would've used it on me instead of hauling ass like he did."

"I already searched it," Bill said as they stepped off the road. "No guns."

He shone his light in the cab before opening the driver's door.

"Do your thing, bro."

Camp handed the gun to Bill, slid into the driver's seat, and examined the ignition.

Bill handed the axe to Jim, and they stood guard while Camp went to work, Jim watching the road while Camp tore into the ignition, cursing, grumbling, nearly leaping out of his skin when the Jeep roared to life.

Then they were in the Jeep, racing back to the lodge.

The first thing Bill noticed when they entered the clearing at the end of The Devil's Tail Road was light falling from the lodge's door onto the porch.

"Shit!" He pointed to the open front door. "Something's happened."

Passing his lopsided Mustang, Camp skidded to a halt in front of the lodge. They all got out, ran to the porch, and up the steps.

They found Casper spread out on the floor inside, split from head to chest, his right arm hacked off at the elbow. A river of blood stretching from his open chest, across the wood floor, under the sofa.

Bill turned away quickly, struggling with the reflex that threatened to eject his last meal. After a brief struggle, he won.

"Fuck *me*," Camp said, staring bug-eyed at Casper's corpse.

Jim rushed past Camp and Bill, nearly tripping over Casper's body before he could stop. His face went white, then he leaned forward and added to the mess.

Bill saw the pink end of a hotdog poking out of the steaming puddle next to Casper like a fingertip, and felt his gorge rise again.

"Yo," Camp said, and tugged at his arm.

"What?" Bill's voice was weak.

Then he saw what Camp pointed at.

Ryan, lying on the floor by the flickering fireplace. Blood leaked from his split scalp, but he was breathing.

"This poor bastard sure can take a beating," Camp said, bending down and rolling Ryan onto his back. "Like a fucking Timex."

He gave Ryan's cheek a light slap, and when that didn't wake him, a hard one.

Ryan groaned, but did not stir.

Jim knelt next to him. "Ryan, wake up. Ryan!"

"Shut up and grab his legs," Camp said, and Jim did, his cheeks flushing red.

They carried him to the sofa, Camp carefully stepping over the tacky river of blood running from Casper's split chest.

Bill made a quick search of the room, found a trail of bloody boot-prints, big boot-prints, leading into the hall-way. He followed the trail with his eyes, and saw the back door standing open.

"He's your publisher," Bill said to Jim. "You get to babysit him."

Camp followed Bill to the back door. "This is going to put a serious crimp in next year's publication schedules," he said, following Bill into the dark.

The bloody boot-prints disappeared in the dust behind the lodge.

"What do you think?" Bill asked.

"I think if we had half a brain between us we'd be driving out of here by now," Camp said. "Since we don't, let's start with the cabins."

Bill nodded, gave Camp his gun, and followed him to the nearest cabin. Resting the heavy axe over his shoulder, he pushed the door open. It swung all the way in, slamming against the wall. He moved the flashlight's beam through the dark room, but found no one. Not satisfied, Bill stepped inside and walked to the bed. He flipped it over. Nothing beneath it. After checking inside the shower, he left the cabin and checked the next.

Two next two cabins were empty as well.

The door of the fourth was already partway open, giving him a sliver of a view. Nothing caught his eye, so he pushed it in and stepped over the threshold.

It flew back at him without warning and slammed into his face. The axe slid from his hand and he stumbled backward, sprawling to the dust.

There was a cold pain in Bill's head as it struck the flat of the axe's blade, a loud ringing in his ears. Bill shook his head to clear the stars, and when his vision cleared, he found Yohan standing above him, raising Bill's axe with both hands.

Camp's gun boomed, and Bill saw a muzzle flash behind Yohan.

Yohan howled and fell to his knees, dropping the axe.

Bill rolled aside and heard the blade strike dirt where his head had been only a second before. A moment later he was on his feet again.

Yohan squirmed in the dirt, moaned and clutched at his knee. Blood ran from between his fingers.

Camp knelt down beside Yohan and pressed the

muzzle of his gun into the loose flesh under his chin. "Where are they?"

"I don't know what you're taking about," Yohan said.

Camp withdrew the gun and brought his fist down against Yohan's jaw.

"What did you do with them?" Bill asked.

"Fuck you!"

Camp stood, aimed, and fired.

Dirt exploded from the ground a few inches above Yohan's head.

"Susan and Heather," Camp shouted. "Where are they?"

"I didn't do anything with them." Yohan stared defiantly into the barrel of Camp's gun.

"I think I know," Bill said, and Camp looked up, his gun still trained on Yohan.

"That trail by the lake. Someone didn't want us using it."

Camp nodded. "Get up."

"I can't," Yohan said. "You blew my fucking knee out!"

"You'll manage," Bill said. "Or I can drag you all the way down there."

Somehow, Yohan did manage, hissing in pain as he pushed himself to his feet.

"Jim," Bill shouted.

"You get him?" Jim stepped onto the porch, then started toward them.

"Stay with Ryan. Try to wake his ass up." Bill shouted. "We're going to find the girls."

Jim walked back to the porch and vanished inside the lodge without a word.

"Move," Camp said.

"Where you think we're going?" Yohan said, his voice arrogant even in defeat.

"The lake for starters." He pushed Yohan forward. "Now, get moving before I let Camp shoot you again."

THE NEW HACKS

From The Buttercup of Doom Podcast:

03:21 Kelli Owen: *So, The New Hacks ... really people! Fucking really?*

(long moment of silence, then an audible thump)

03:26 Kelli Owen: *Sorry listeners, had to take a little break. Seriously though, shit like this is why we need legal weed in this state! Unless you've been living under a rock, you've heard about the Hack's Club Massacre. We lost important people there. I lost friends there! The whole thing is still kinda fresh for most of us, and there's a group of jack-asses already trying to publicize themselves as The New Hacks. They have a website, a Facebook page, a message board, and a goddamn mission statement ... Out with the old, in with the new.*

04:16 Audio Clip: *Legends are fine ... we all love a legend ... but there are so many dinosaurs in this business that publishers, reviewers, and quite frankly readers don't have the time or inclination to give new talent a chance. So, no, I won't apologize for celebrating the forced retirement of so many old guard authors.*

04:50 Kelli Owen: *(growling noise) I won't name and shame them here because they don't deserve the publicity, but you can find out who they are with a simple Internet search. They should be aware that editors, reviewers, and quite frankly readers, are paying attention and staying away in droves.*

CHAPTER 16

Surprise on Dead Bear Trail

"You strung that dead bear up didn't you?" Bill said to Yohan, who took a limping lead down the trail. "When Ryan found it, I thought it was your way of trying to scare us so Susan wouldn't fire you."

"You're talking crazy," Yohan said.

"I think," Camp said, "maybe he just wanted to keep us off that trail."

"Keep moving," Bill said to Yohan, who had stopped and turned to stare at them.

"Is Michael down there too?" Camp asked. "Or did you just kill him outright like Tracy and Casper and leave him in the woods?"

Bill bet on the latter. Michael was most likely dead somewhere. He wondered if anyone would ever find the body.

The girls though … Bill thought Yohan would want to keep them for a while. He hoped so anyway. If there was a chance either of them were still alive, maybe he could quit feeling so guilty about leaving them behind.

At the lake now. The night had cleared, though more clouds loomed, manifesting as wide swaths of pitch blackness breaking up the stars. Moonlight illuminated a shape on the granite slab ahead.

"Why did you kill Tracy? She put up too much of a fight? Did she tell you what a disgusting fuck you are maybe, and you just lost it?" This, Bill said, expecting nothing more than Yohan's sulking silence.

"I didn't," Yohan said. "I found her like that, but I didn't kill her."

"Who did, then?" Camp asked, punctuating the question by jabbing his gun's muzzle into Yohan's back. "The same guy who slashed my tires? Or the same guy who stole the battery out of the lodge's radio?"

"Fuck you," Yohan said, and Camp kicked his bad knee out from under him.

Yohan screamed and landed sprawled out in the dirt.

Bill took a moment to enjoy Yohan's suffering. Seeing that big, dumb bastard weeping in the dirt did his heart good. Bending, he seized the man by the back of his shirt, and yanked him up.

"You shouldn't have done that," he said. "Camp loves that car."

"So what if I did *that*," Yohan said, shoving Bill's hands away, stumbling forward. "Cutting a few tires and breaking that bitch's radio ain't killin'."

They were there now. Bill saw Tracy's body lying like a chunk of cougar bait, cooling by the lake. Someone had cleared away the camouflage Ryan and Jim had put up. Dead Bear Trail opened to them, inviting and forbidding at the same time. He shined his light down it, but the illumination petered out before revealing much.

"Cut the shit," Bill said, shoving Yohan into the mouth of the trail. "Go on now."

Yohan led them silently down long straight stretches and many twisting curves. He beat a slow, limping pace and kept his silence. He didn't slow as they approached blind turns. After what Bill judged to be about twenty minutes, he had second thoughts. But they kept moving.

Yohan rounded another corner, then backpedaled, screaming as Bill caught a fistful of his jacket and pushed him forward again.

The headless bear hung between the trees, continuing its slow return to the earth. Its stench was worse than ever.

"I'll be dipped in shit," Yohan whispered.

"Keep moving," Camp said, then prodded Yohan with the gun.

Yohan glared over his shoulder, but moved along, squeezing between the hanging bear and the nearest tree.

Bill and Camp followed him deeper into the dark.

***

Stumbling through the trees, Heather and Susan clutched each other. Thoroughly lost, but being lost was a minor concern. They had escaped.

"Susan, we can stop for a minute."

"Yes."

They felt blindly for a bare spot on the ground, then sat on a cushion of pine needles and dead moss.

Heather looked up. "I can't see the sky. Do you know where we are?"

"No," Susan said. "Hold on a minute."

She shifted away from Heather, leaned over for a moment, then sat up again. A second later a pop and fizzle, the smell of sulfur, and a small light filled their dark world.

Heather squinted against the glare, and when her eyes adjusted, she saw Susan clutching a book of matches in one hand. In the other she held a burning paper match between the thumb and forefinger. Clearing a spot on the forest floor, Susan built a small mound of moss, needles, and a few twigs, and touched the match to it just before the flame reached her finger tips.

The circle of light around them grew.

"Ryan told me if I got lost out here to remember one thing."

"What was that," Heather asked.

"No matter which way you walk, you'll come out of the woods. You'll find a road, the clearing, or the lake. As long as you're not walking downhill. Downhill is a dead end into the canyon."

The feeble light of their fire already fading, Susan whispered, "Which way?"

"Which way do we go?" Susan whispered.

Heather tried to find their back-trail, but could not. She scanned every direction, but each way looked the same. She stood, picked a direction, and pointed.

"Are you sure?"

"No."

"What if we find…," Susan seemed unable to finish the thought aloud.

"Then we run like hell," Heather said. "Or we'll die."

Jim could not stay inside the lodge with Casper's corpse, so he carried Ryan onto the porch and set him in the porch swing hanging from the eaves.

He'd tried shaking Ryan awake to no effect. So he waited. If Bill and Camp came back, please, God, let Heather and Susan be with them, before Ryan woke, then he'd just have to carry him to the Jeep.

Ryan gave a low groan, then stirred. Shortly after, he opened his eyes and blinked.

"Ryan," Jim said, leaning over him, relieved to see the recognition in the man's eyes.

He tried to sit up, and Jim helped him.

"I'm alive," Ryan said.

"Yeah," Jim said. "But you keep getting beat up."

"Susan and Heather?" There was a pleading note in his voice.

"I don't know. Bill and Camp have Yohan. If Heather and Susan are alive, they'll bring them back." Jim scanned the area by the far cabins, hoping to see them all coming.

He didn't.

Ryan grabbed the front of Jim's shirt, pulling him close. "Which way'd they go?"

"By the lake, I think. What …?"

"No! They shouldn't be down there. They're no match for him!"

Jim pried Ryan's hand from his shirt, knelt down and took Ryan by the shoulders, and shook him. "They have Yohan. He can't hurt anyone else."

Ryan stood, stumbled, grabbed the porch's banister for support. "You don't understand! We were wrong. It wasn't Yohan!"

"What?"

"Yohan didn't kill Tracy. He didn't kill Casper!" Ryan closed his eyes, seemingly fighting off a wave of dizziness. When he spoke again, he was calmer, but no less urgent. "It wasn't Yohan. Someone else is out there."

Tension built in Bill's chest as they continued down Dead Bear Trail.

The terrain beyond the bear was a rough monotony of long stretches, broken up by sharp turns. The only thing different was the downward pitch as they entered the canyon that epitomized the wilderness that was Mount Misery.

Despite himself, Yohan had begun to talk to them, his tone decidedly docile. He was getting used to the idea that Bill and Camp were in charge of this expedition.

Between helpful scraps like *watch your footing here* and *duck that limb* he rambled.

"Been more'n dozen years since I've been s'far down this trial. If we don't turn back we'll be at the bottom of the canyon before light."

Bill ignored Him. He was not interested in holding a conversation with the bastard.

"How much farther?" Camp asked.

"'Til what?" Yohan said, and chuckled lightly.

Rain pattered against the canopy of evergreen boughs overhead, but did not filter down to them. It would take a heavier downpour to breach their cover.

"Don't know what you expect to find," Yohan said. "I

didn't pack your women down here. I didn't kill your friends."

"Shut up and walk," Bill said.

Yohan did.

It wasn't long before he spoke again though.

"Well, that's new."

Bill directed the beam of his light where Yohan had stopped, hands on his hips.

A second trail broke from the main trail, leading into more darkness.

"Where does it go?" Camp said.

"Would you believe me if I said I had no idea?"

"No," Camp said. "You're going to show us."

"Yohan sighed and led them down the rough, narrow trail, no longer descending, but on a tilted flat.

The beam of light dimmed. Bill slapped the flashlight against his palm, and followed Camp and Yohan down the trail. They found the end in less than a minute, and the shabbiest cabin he'd ever seen waiting at its end, squat, leaning, constructed of mismatched planks framed by trees and warped vertical boards. The ceiling was strips of wood and rusted pieces of tin, covered mostly by dead and dying evergreen limbs. In place of a door was a filthy, rotting curtain of old canvas.

"This," Bill said, "must be your home away from home. You first. Go in."

"I've never seen this place in my life," Yohan said. But he did as he was told, walking to the cabin's canted face and pushing the canvas aside.

The stench inside was breathtaking. A quick sweep of his flashlight revealed the source of the stench. Dead animals, deer, rabbits, and what looked like part of a small bear, covered the dirt floor at one end. Their skins hung from the walls, bones sat in a mound, and a heap of flesh and organs sat on a chestnut pelt. An assortment of knives, an axe, a machete, and a rifle so rusted it would never fire again, sat on a small, stout table. Next to a bare mattress, filthy and sprouting springs and stuffing, there was a chair.

In the chair sat a skeleton dressed in plaid and wool. It sat with its hands folded in its lap, grinning, as if happy for the company. Camp's Jet cap sat on its head.

Susan and Heather were not there.

"Jesus in heaven," Yohan said, and backed toward the door.

Bill grabbed him.

"You let me go now," Yohan shouted, a high, panicked shout. His air of calm, country superiority was gone.

"Where are they," Camp said, and pointed the gun at Yohan's face.

But Yohan seemed not to care. He fought to get out of Bill's grip. "I told you I don't know!"

"Tell me something, Yohan. Why are you so scared now?" He nodded toward their grinning host, sitting impassively as ever. "You know him?"

At these words Yohan's struggle ended. He regarded Bill and Camp in turn, then faced the skeleton again and shivered.

"I know him," Yohan said. "And I think I know who killed your friends."

"Talk," Camp said. He relieved the skeleton of his Jets cap, regarded it with a frown, then rolled it up and stuffed it into his back pocket.

Yohan talked.

"I never did like Sheriff Randy Frye," Yohan said. "And he never did like me. We bumped heads from time to time, but was never nothing serious. He liked to hound me, but never had anything to run me in with.

"He had a boy named Rex. Twice as big as any other kid his age and with a head like a basketball. Huge head. I heard there wasn't anything inside it but water and a brain the size of a walnut. He had red hair, but it was mostly gone by the time he was ten years old.

"That boy was the worst kind of retard. Stupid like an animal. Great big green eyes that stared at you, like he wanted to eat you ... what?"

"You're an asshole," Camp informed him.

Yohan shrugged his shoulders and continued.

"Like I said, the sheriff and me didn't like each other, but we never had big trouble until he heard me talking about his boy. I was in the old Up & Up Tavern down at Pomeroy, having a drink, and in comes old Mr. Williams, I was friends with his boy, Drew, and Mr. Williams was cussing out Frye real good. Frye'd impounded his truck that morning for bad tags.

"So I bought him a beer, and we had us a good time ripping up the star toting numb-fuck.

"I was remembering his boy because I'd seen him sitting on the sidewalk in front of the candy store that morning, staring at me while I walked by. I told Mr. Williams I thought the unnatural little retard belonged in a sideshow.

"That was when Sheriff Frye pulled me off my stool. He'd been standing there and listening for a while.

"I was good and drunk by then, wasn't in my right mind you know? I hit him, and that was that. He beat the crap out of me in front of everyone there and cuffed me.

"I didn't spend more than a few months in jail, but when I got out I lost my right to carry firearms. Lost my right to vote. That pompous bastard made me a fool in front of everyone, then turned me into a second-class citizen.

"Was about a year later, I was out here, down in this canyon, hunting with Drew. I wasn't allowed anymore, but I didn't let it stop me.

"These woods are big, and I hardly ever met another hunter out in them, but that day Drew and me ran across Randy Frye, taking his retard Rex out hunting.

"There was no way I was going to prison …"

"So you killed them," Bill said. "Left them out here to rot."

Yohan shook his head. "Just the Sheriff. His retard ran away."

"What happened to Rex?" camp asked.

Yohan didn't answer. He stood, back to the canvas door, his eyes drawn again to the man he'd killed those years ago. A dead man in a flannel coat and fur hat, grinning his unshakable grin.

Been waiting for you, Yohan. Knew you'd come back some day.

The voice, nothing but a product of Bill's overactive imagination, a writer's imagination, made him shiver.

The ripping sound caught him by surprise, and he jerked his head back to Yohan.

Yohan's chest arched out, his face turned to the ceiling. He began to shake, then grunted, and a jet of blood flew from his open mouth.

Then the tip of a large blade burst through his chest, cracking through ribs, popping one of the buttons off his shirt. He flew backward, out of the cabin, through the air into the darkness with the blood-soaked canvas following him like the tail of a kite.

A monster of a man stood in the doorway, facing them. Years of filth caked the disintegrating pants stretched over legs like tree trunks, and a shawl of mismatched pelts draped his shoulders and chest. The rotting face of a bear covered the man's large head like a hood. Large green eyes glared through the holes where the bears eyes should have been.

The hulking man stepped into his home and faced the invaders.

Bill stumbled back, his ass hitting the table, and grabbed blindly for one of the weapons on it. He brought up a large rusted hunting knife and threw it.

His aim was good. The knife's blade sank into the fur draped chest. The green-eyed beast did not slow. He advanced on Bill with measured steps.

"*Motherfucker,*" Camp screamed, and fired his remaining rounds.

Blood splashed from the beast's pelt-draped shoulder, bits of flesh flew from his arm. Something clear and thick splashed from a smoking hole in the bear mask. He stumbled, and Bill shouted in savage, adrenaline primed triumph.

But the monster did not fall. He stepped forward again and turned to face Camp. A swing of his machete brought

Camp down in two pieces, the top half screaming, the bottom half kicking as nerves fired and muscles spasmed for the last time.

Bill screamed, shock and rage, and grabbed the axe sitting on the table. Raising it overhead, he lunged.

*Foul Play Suspected in Disappearance
of Sheriff Randy Frye And Son.*

*The search for Garfield County Sheriff Randy Frye and his
son, Rex Frye, continues into its second week, but the Search
and Rescue says the prospects of finding the missing man and
his son are grim.*

*"We know he was on a weekend hunting trip with his boy, but
we don't know where. There's a lot of ground to cover still, and
the longer we search, the more likely it is we'll never find him."*

*Sheriff Frye's truck was found concealed in a wooded valley
near the Stentz Springs area Tuesday morning, fueling
speculation that foul play was involved. The search for Randy
and Rex Frye is now centered around Stentz Springs.*

*Leading the investigation, acting Sheriff Robert Lewis admits
there is little hope.*

"We have his truck but nothing else. We do have a local man in custody for questioning, but he hasn't been any help to us yet. If we don't find them, dead or alive, before the snow falls, we may never know what happened. We have another week, two tops."

Lewis went on to say that the chances of surviving a winter stranded or lost in the Blues were little or none.

Pastor Maurice Broaddus of the Pomeroy Congregational Church will lead a prayer vigil, beginning tonight at 7:00 PM.

CHAPTER 17

Blind Run

They heard the gunshots, screams so distant they were barely audible, and they bolted down the steps.

Ryan saw the idling Jeep and paused at the bottom of the steps. The temptation to grab Jim by the back of the neck and drag him to it, and at least save their own lives, was almost too strong an impulse to resist. But that opportunity expired as Jim passed him, running past cabins, toward the lake trail.

I could still go, he thought. *It would be the smart thing to do.*

But he only stood there, turning first to watch Jim passing the last cabin, then turning back to the headlights of the idling Jeep.

Light, safely, escape.

Darkness, danger, death.

Ryan chose.

Heather and Susan stopped.

"Camp?" Susan said.

"I think so." Heather tried to gauge the distance of the shots, but couldn't. Only the direction. A slight correction would take them that way.

So now what?

If Camp was that way, Bill would be too. Maybe Jim and Ryan.

The scream after the shots had been unnerving. If they followed the gunfire, they could be running toward danger. But they had to do it. Their friends were somewhere down that dark trail.

Susan was no help. She only stood, silent, motionless, waiting.

"Let's go," Heather said, and they ran toward what she hoped would be friendly faces, not the giant in the bear face mask.

Please, God, not him.

Bill dropped the axe and fixed the beam of light on the freak before him, shocked that he was still alive.

Rex had dropped, fallen through the crude doorway and landed with the thud of a small tree.

With a knife in his chest, and three bullets in him, the creature, who could only have been Yohan's Rex, had kept coming. The blunt end of the axe had done what the bullets had not.

Bill's swing had caught Rex on the forehead with a splintering crunch. He'd expected the killer to keep coming anyway, to take him apart like he had Camp.

Standing in the doorway of that rank little shack, Bill was too frightened to take a step towards him.

Move you numb fuck!

And finally, he did, slowly, carefully, stepping over Rex's legs as he passed through the doorway, then made his way around the huge man and onto the trail.

Expecting with every step to feel the pressure of Rex's huge fists closing around his ankle.

It didn't happen. Rex lay still.

Stunned or dead?

Bill fought the impulse to bolt. He had to make sure, or the fear of not knowing would follow him every step of the way back.

Bill bent, poised to spring and run at the first sign of life from the monster that Yohan had made, grabbed the fur of Rex's bear head mask, and pulled. The mask was a tight fit, not wanting to give up its secrets. Bill tugged harder, the light aimed, shaking, at Rex's head.

The mask pulled free, dropping Bill on his ass. He found his feet with a speed born of fear, and shined the light in Rex's face.

"Motherfucker," he gasped, staring down at a face the likes of which he'd only seen in the cheesiest movies.

This face was not latex and karo-syrup blood. It was real.

Large, pale, bald but for a few clumps of long red hair, Rex's face was a tangle of scare tissue, a flat, flap of a nose, two rows of large ugly teeth, and green eyes. Large green eyes.

A small hole above one temple leaked a sticky, clear fluid. The center of his forehead was pushed in, creased by the blow of the axe.

Dead, Bill thought. *I killed him.*

Then the great green eyes blinked.

They found a trail, an honest to God trail, and paused so Susan could light another match. With eyes that had almost adjusted to the dark, the meager light seemed like a flare. Only feet away, a tangle of deadfalls blocked the path. The other way was wide open.

The match singed Susan's fingertips. She shook it out and they followed the path.

Moonlight filtered through the treetops, casting a defining light on the trail as they hurried down it. Shadows reached out, gray shapes of swaying and reaching arms. Susan hoped they were just tree limbs.

And then they saw the end of the trail, moonlight falling over the ground beyond the trees.

"Almost there," Susan said, as much for her own benefit as Heather's.

"I see it," Heather said between huffing breaths. "Getting brighter."

Then a stink surrounded them like fog, killing the pleasant scent of pine and wildflowers. A stink like puke, shit, and soured meat enclosed them as Susan tripped.

What is that smell? Heather felt a sour reflux at the back of her throat and knew she'd vomit if she didn't get away soon.

Almost there. Her thought echoed Susan's hopeful words.

Heather saw the gray, bobbing shape that was Susan fall to the blackness of the ground. There was a grunt and the hard sound of impact, the crack of a breaking bone, and Susan's scream.

Heather put the brakes on, grabbed at the limbs slapping her shoulders to keep from joining Susan in the dirt, the smell getting stronger, filling her nose. The rotting stench of death.

"Susan?" She took a tentative step forward, another, and met resistance. Something soft.

Susan groaned. "My arm," she said. "I think I broke my arm."

Heather knelt down. "It's okay. I'll help you." She reached out to help Susan up, and jerked away when her hand sank into something cold, wet, and slimy. Her hand popped loose with a squelch, and the unbearable stench strengthened, like something made solid.

"Heather?" Susan's voice came from farther down the trail.

"Oh no!"

Heather wiped her hand across pine needles and dirt, trying to scour the tacky wetness from it, then leaned over and vomited. Three voiding spasms shot from the bottom of her stomach, out through her mouth and nose. The last, dry and hot, felt like it had torn something loose inside. It was like vomiting sand.

"Heather?"

"I'm here," Heather wiped her mouth across her sleeve. "Give me a second."

Susan began to whimper.

When Heather felt safe to move again, she stood, found the edge of the trail, and stepped around the body. Limbs scratched at her, drawing stinging lines across patches of exposed skin. She didn't care. The pain took her focus off the smell.

Susan lay a few feet away, and Heather knelt before her. "Do you have any matches left?"

"In my pocket."

"I have to see who it is," Heather said. She patted her hands up and down Susan's legs, felt a small square bulge. She didn't want to harm Susan, so she carefully slipped her hand into a pocket, worked it slowly inside, then pulled the matchbook out.

"Hurry," Susan said. "I want to get out of here."

"Okay."

Heather crawled a few feet, until the gray shape of the body was visible in the darkness again, and lit a match.

And then wished she hadn't.

"Oh," she sighed, then dropped the match and turned away. "It's Michael."

Poor Michael, open from crotch to neck; most of his insides hanging out.

Poor Michael. But a part of her was relieved. She'd half expected to see Jim's face, eyes dry and staring in terminal shock.

She went to Susan, helped her up as gently as she could.

Once upright she was able to stand on her own. Heather thanked God it wasn't one of her legs.

But their progress would be slow from here. The woods would have them for a while longer.

They started down the trail, this time at a slow walk, and something came stomping up the trail toward them.

***

Jim rushed past the outhouse, willing himself to slow his suicidal pace.

Shit, I'm running blind.

Then he heard another scream from the woods to his right.

A woman's scream. A scream of pain, not terror.

He stopped at the edge of a trail he'd explored the day before, and thought he heard voices.

A moment later Ryan stood by his side, bent over, hands on his knees and puffing like an asthmatic.

Jim remembered Ryan's broken nose, the blow he'd taken to his head, and felt guilty for forcing the insane pace on him.

"What is it?" Ryan asked after catching his breath.

Jim pointed down the trail. "The girls," he said. "I think."

Ryan stared down the trail, then toward the far end of the lake, then back down trail again.

They listened, heard nothing.

Jim considered calling out to them, then quickly reconsidered. Instead he stepped onto the trail and began to jog.

They didn't have to go far.

Two shapes walking side by side emerged from the darkness, and stopped.

"Heather? Susan?" Jim said.

"Jim," Heather called out, and half the fear he'd carried with him fell away.

They found each other, held each other, and he found more comfort than he would have thought possible in her arms.

"Michael's dead," Heather said. "We found him back there."

"Ouch, careful."

Jim turned and found Ryan, one arm around Susan's waist, helping her along.

"I think it's broken," Susan said

Each step brought a gasp of pain from her, and when they were close enough to be more than gray blurs, Jim saw her favoring her right arm.

"We have to get out of here," Ryan said.

"Camp and Bill?"

Ryan did not answer.

Jim understood, and agreed.

Bill and Camp were probably dead too, or so lost they would never be able to find them alone.

It was time to go.

Minutes later they stepped back into moonlight, and started up the lake trail, toward the lodge. Toward escape.

At the far end of the lake, someone burst though the mouth of the last trail.

Jim turned and squinted.

A blinding beam of light fell over them.

Behind the light, Bill's voice screamed, "Run!"

With Ryan supporting Susan on one side, her arm thrown

over his shoulder, they reached the top of the lake trail just as Bill caught up to them.

Bill held the light on the trail a few feet ahead of them, its beam darker now that it was even a few minutes before. In his other hand, something foul hung from fisted fingers like a cannibal's prize.

"Where's Camp?" Heather called back over her shoulder. Bill was only steps behind her, but with the stomping of feet, the heavy breathing of people who made their livings sitting on their asses, and Susan's groans and cries of pain as her broken arm jostled, she had to shout.

"Dead," Bill said, slowing his pace to match as he sidled next to her. "Yohan too."

He looked back over his shoulder, trained the light on the trail behind them.

It was empty.

He slowed, moving the beam farther down the trail, but no one followed.

"We can walk now," he said. "I don't think he's following."

He didn't have to tell them twice. They stopped where the trail opened onto the clearing and waited for Bill.

They were out of the woods now, but the open air was still far too dark. The clouds had swallowed the stars and moon. Heather smelled rain in the air. It would start soon.

"Who is he?" Jim asked. His eyes flashed down to the thing hanging from Bill's fist. "What does he want?"

"His name is Rex Frye," Bill said, then held up the bear mask.

Ryan's eyes widened and he backed away a step.

Heather flinched, turned her eyes from it.

"He's an animal," Bill continued. "And as far as I can tell, he wants to kill us."

They moved as a group, not running, but not loafing, toward the lodge, and the waiting Jeep. Bill kept a constant watch on the path behind them as he relayed Yohan's story.

Ryan listened to Bill's story with a growing sense of horror. It took all his self-control not to sprint to the Jeep.

Three shots, one to the head, and the blow Bill had delivered with the blunt end of the axe, should have killed him. The monster he called Rex. Ryan mastered, barely, the impulse to ask Bill why the hell he hadn't picked up the axe while Rex was down and finished the job.

Obviously, Bill had thought Rex was dead, or he wouldn't have had the guts to unmask him. And seeing those big green eyes blink, then focus on him as the freakish man's chest heaved a great breath of air, well that would have freaked Ryan out too.

Still, freaked or not, Ryan didn't think he'd have been able to stop swinging the axe until there was nothing left of the monster's head.

"Alive or not, I don't think he'd be able to follow you far," Ryan said, more to convince himself than anyone else.

Bill nodded. "I still think we should get out of here. Now."

The others agreed. They piled into the Jeep, Jim and Heather in the back, Susan up front, in the passenger's seat.

Ryan and Bill stood for a moment, both eyeing the driver's seat, but neither moving toward it.

"Go ahead," Bill said. "You drive." He walked to the rear, opened the hatch, and climbed into the cramped space behind the back seat. He rolled the hatch's window down, then pulled it closed.

Ryan hurried to the driver's seat, and slammed the door closed behind himself.

"No, Bill," Heather said. "We'll make room up here."

"Don't worry about it," Bill said. "Let's just go."

Ryan shifted into first gear, careful not to stall the Jeep. The cluster of wires hanging from the ignition told him it was hot-wired, and he didn't want to fry himself trying to restart the damned Jeep if he killed it.

Headlights drilled through the blackness of woods-enclosed road, but the light did not comfort him. It only sharpened the darkness around them.

He drove slowly at first, itching to go balls to the wall, but not wanting to beat Bill up with the rough road. When Bill himself told Ryan to put his fucking foot down, he did.

Ten miles an hour slowly became twenty. When the first rough patch slammed the Jeep, making Bill curse and Susan cry out in pain, clutching her broken arm to her chest, he backed it down to fifteen.

Not as fast as Yohan had driven, but Yohan knew

every twist and bump in this road. Still too fast, but not near fast enough.

For no reason he could pin down, Ryan suddenly thought of all those rare, autographed books sitting abandoned in the lodge, and felt a moment of raw anger at Rex for having to abandon them.

Stupid, he knew, but real.

Stress does weird shit to you.

He slowed a little, rounding one of a hundred sharp curves on this godforsaken road, then put his foot down again, watching the darkness to his left. Almost expecting someone to jump out at him.

"Watch out!"

Ryan didn't know who had said it. Several voices seemed to be shouting at once. He whipped his head forward again, and went cold. Rex stood in the merging cones of light, holding the axe they'd split wood with the night before. It looked very small in Rex's hands.

The glow falling across his chest lit him from the neck down. His face was in darkness, but Ryan thought he saw twin flashes of green where his eyes would have been.

"Stop!" Jim screamed behind him.

Fuck that, Ryan thought, and pressed the gas pedal to the floor.

Rex leaped to their right, and Ryan had just enough time to marvel at how something so fucking huge could move that quickly before he saw what lay across the road behind where Rex had stood.

He screamed and stomped the brake pedal, but it was too late.

The trunk of the tree that lay across the road was old wood, bald and probably long dead. But it was enough.

They slammed into it, and Ryan thought the shock of the steering wheel striking his chest would be enough to stop his heart.

Screams behind him, screams beside him, the crash and squeal of metal. Then the groan of the Jeep's twisted frame as it settled.

After a few moments of pitch-black darkness and silence, Ryan realized the impact had not killed him after all. What he saw next made him wish it had.

———

When Susan opened her eyes she was outside again, not in the Jeep's cab, but lying face down on the bent ruins of its hood. For one horrible moment she thought she was paralyzed, but then, with great effort, she turned onto her side. Her broken arm still hurt, but that muted pain was just one of many.

The ringing in her ears and the screams of her Hacks, the ones who still lived, merged into a hellish chorus.

Rex stepped from the darkness, out of the woods he'd vanished into moments before, and reached for her. One hand, huge and strong, grabbed her throat while the other pinned her down.

A new wrenching pain exploded in her neck, down her spine. Muscle stretched, skin split, vertebrae cracked and separated. With a final crunch of bone, all of her pain ceased.

Susan was weightless, flying, spinning through the air.

Into oblivion.

———

They ran together, finding each other, taking hold of hands and arms as if by instinct. Heather knew if they separated, they were dead.

She recognized them each by their individual sounds. Jim's winded panting, Bill cursing as he stumbled and barely avoided dragging them all down, Ryan by his nasal grunts of negation.

"Nuh, nuh, nuh!"

Beneath these sounds, Susan's last scream echoed in her mind, and Heather was aware, vaguely, that she was crying.

They seemed to run for hours. Getting nowhere. She hoped whoever was leading the group knew where the turns were, otherwise they were likely to kill themselves running blindly into the dense woods that bordered the narrow road.

Every now and then she heard, or thought she heard, something close behind them. Something big stomping the ground, snapping low boughs.

A sudden, brilliant flash of light bleached out the night, revealing the end of The Devil's Tail Road, now very close. The light vanished, lingering for a moment on Heather's retinas. Then came the boom of thunder, very close, startling a scream out of her

What had been a sporadic, light sprinkling, became a torrent. Even with the cover overhead, they were soaked in seconds.

Then they were free of The Devil's Tail Road's wooded throat. The quality of the darkness changed, a ghost of moonlight shimmered behind clouds, teasing her.

"Come on," Bill said, and she felt herself pulled in a new direction.

Heather let herself be led, and moments later the rain no longer fell on her, though she could still hear it coming down hard on the roof of the cabin they'd pulled her into. Then a door slammed, and the sounds of the storm were muted.

"Get the blinds." Jim's voice, scared and small. Still under his control, but just barely.

Someone climbed on the bed, the frame squeaked under their weight, and she heard the whisper of canvas as they drew the blinds down. Someone else did the same for the small front window.

Then there was light. The flickering light of a gas flame from the fixture on the other side of the door frame.

Bill stood, squinting as he adjusted the flame down, then rushed to the door and locked it.

Ryan rushed past her and stripped the blanket from the bed, then pulled a folding knife from his pocket, thumbed out a short blade, and began cutting the blanket in half.

Jim was in the corner of the cabin that served as a kitchen, pulling drawers out. Looking for a knife, she thought.

Heather stood while they scrambled, wanting to do something, but unable to think of what to do.

The familiar woozy sensation came over her, starting at the back of her head and washing over her like something cold and thick.

Not now, she begged. *Not here.*

But it came anyway, and she knew from experience there was no halting it. The only thing to do was find something soft to lie on, or land on, and hope it came and went quickly.

Hope she didn't wake up to find Camp, Tracy, Michael, Casper, and Susan waiting for her on the other side of that thin, receding veil.

Heather stepped toward the narrow bed, her legs going weak, rubbery. She stumbled, did not feel pain as her knees struck the cabin's hard wood floor. She fell forward and caught the edge of the bed and dragged herself forward, then collapsed. She'd made it halfway onto the bed. That would have to be good enough.

She waited for the darkness, hearing the men's voices, dimly, sounding half concerned, half annoyed.

She did not wait long.

"Fuck," Bill said, but did not quite dare shout.

Jim abandoned his search for knives, or anything they could use as a weapon, an ice pick or meat fork would have been just fine, to see what Bill was cussing about. He saw Heather collapsed, half on, half off the bed.

"Jesus, Heather! Are you okay?" A half-dozen steps took him to her side.

Ryan, draping one half of the bed sheet over the blinds on the front window to eliminate any glow the low light cast through the canvas, looked over his shoulder. He echoed Bill's sentiment, then turned his attention back to the window.

The window above the bed was already shaded. Jim hoped like hell the extra layer of cloth would do the trick.

Any light that shone through those windows would be a beacon.

Jim and Bill lifted Heather onto the bed. She'd begun muttering in her sleep again. She looked at peace, but Jim knew it was an illusion. She was not at peace, she had only exchanged one nightmare for another.

"She gonna be okay?" Bill asked.

"Yeah," Jim said. "I think so."

"I had a friend who spent some time in Kuwait during the Gulf War. Came back with PTSD triggered narcolepsy." Bill gave Jim a grim look. "This looks a lot like that. You certain she'll be okay?"

"I'm not certain any of us will be okay," Jim snapped, then in a tone of forced calm, "this has happened twice since we've come here, and yes, stress brings it on. Both times she came around within a few minutes."

This seemed to mollify Bill. Nodding, he gave Heather a final cold, appraising look, and sighed. "We're going to have to lay low until morning," Bill said. "The only chance we have of getting out of here is daylight, and even then, I don't like our chances."

We won't last until morning, Jim almost said.

"No," Ryan said suddenly, viciously. "I'm not running."

He bent down and picked up the matted bear mask, probably taken from the headless bear on the trail, Jim realized. Bill must have run the whole way clutching that damn thing in his fist.

"He killed Camp, Bill. He killed your friend. He killed Susan. He killed Tracy, Casper, and Michael." His face, previously pale from blood loss and shock had gone bright red. His eyes were red too; tears still seeped from them.

"Ryan, I saw that thing take a bullet in the head. It barely stunned him. I damn near caved his head in, and that didn't stop him."

"That isn't the bogeyman out there," Ryan said. "It isn't a vampire, or werewolf, or Jason-fucking-Voorhees." He held up the bear's skinned face, gave it a savage shake. "He's flesh and blood. If he's alive, he can die."

"You're not the man who's going to take him out," Jim said. "Neither am I, or Bill."

Ryan turned to Jim, scowling. Blood trickled from his nose again and he wiped at it, spreading red stripes across his face. It looked like war paint to Jim.

"A grizzly bear can die too," Bill said, and pointed at the mask in Ryan's fist. "But that doesn't mean I'm going after one with my bare hands."

"We're unarmed," Jim said, "and he's no ordinary man."

"Bullshit," Ryan said. "We have our brains. We'd better start using them before he comes back and finishes us."

Jim expected another argument from Bill, but none came. He frowned and began to pace.

"If you have a plan," Jim said to Ryan, "you'd better let us in on it."

Bill stared at the floor between his feet while Ryan talked, not interrupting.

He did not like what he heard, but knew it was better than waiting, *hoping*, they could simply hide until morning and survive a mad dash down The Devil's Tail and off of Mount Misery.

Either way, their chances sucked. At least Ryan's way they would be *doing* something.

When Ryan finished, he sat down at the little table, drummed his fingers on the worn surface, and waited.

Jim, sitting on the bed beside Heather, seemed lost in his own thoughts. Then he sighed and said, "Okay."

Bill felt the weight of responsibility shift to him, and didn't like it. He'd stopped pacing, faced the shower stall, saw a very large terrycloth robe hanging from a hook on the wall.

Casper's cabin, he thought, and felt suddenly horrible for the way he'd spoken to the man earlier. He'd arrived, expecting there would be trouble with Casper, if only because there was always trouble with *someone*, and Casper, by reputation alone, seemed most likely.

It had felt good earlier, even under the circumstances, when Casper had challenged his authority and Bill had shut him down. It had, in some way, validated Bill's prejudice.

Bill had not realized until that moment that the validation had been important. It made him feel small, and very petty.

Neither Ryan nor Jim had spoken. Bill knew if he turned around now he'd find them watching him, waiting.

A brief flash of memory, Casper laying in a pool of blood, split almost in half, followed by Camp, chopped in half at the waist, lying on the dirt in that old, derelict cabin, made up his mind.

Bill turned and found them, just as he'd expected, staring at him, waiting.

"Fuck it," Bill said. "Let's do it."

CHAPTER 19

Stairway to Darkness

The first step outside the cabin was the hardest. Ryan knew it would be. Turning out the gas light, killing the comforting glow, unlocking the door, then opening it. Those had been hard. Sticking his head out, the rain and a fall of water running from the roof drenching him in an instant, and half expecting the monster to tear it off before he could even step foot outside. It ran counter to every survival instinct in him, but he did it with only the slightest hesitation.

The clouds had broken up, letting moonlight through at full shine, and that had helped. He could see to the fire ring and beyond. To his right, to the last cabin, but not the trail to the lake. To his left, the mouth of The Devil's Tail Road and the woods.

No hulking giant. No monsters.

"Clear," he whispered over his shoulder, and took a step.

Ryan froze in mid stride, one foot inside, the other hovering over the muddy ground. His heart hammered so hard he could feel it inside his head, like the distant sounding of war drums. His guts turned leaden, heavy, wanting to drag him down, and whatever steel there was in his spine seemed to melt.

When his foot hit the mud with a little *splat*, and nothing happened, he took another step and immersed himself in the night. Jim and Bill followed him out. After another quick scan, they closed the door and ran to the lodge.

Gas light fell through the empty door frame, painting a sharp slab on the porch. Ryan stepped into it gratefully, despite what he knew waited inside. He willed himself not to look at Casper's body, but couldn't escape the smell, the faint ammonia of urine, almost lost under the stronger stench of shit. The body voided its bowels and bladder when it died, a gruesome little factoid Ryan had picked up while reading one manuscript or another.

Strongest of all, something sharp and hot and undeniable.

Ryan walked to the couch, looking down only to locate and avoid the wide streak of drying blood. He stripped the throw blanket from the back of the couch, and turned. He had to look now, but comforted himself with the knowledge that it would be the last time.

Casper barely resembled himself. He was a blood-soaked mannequin, a disregarded prop from a slasher movie. Ryan held his breath, then bent and spread the blanket over him. But he couldn't cover the appalling lake of blood that surrounded the dead man.

"C'mon," Jim said, standing just inside the room, pacing and throwing glances through the door. "Let's hurry."

Bill looked calm, leaning against the wall by the fireplace. He saw the poker that Ryan had dropped. A large nick had been taken out of the metal where he'd blocked Rex's machete. Bill picked it up. He looked much more confident holding it than Ryan had.

Ryan motioned them forward, and preceded them into the hallway.

The back door hung open, so he closed and locked it, then stepped into the kitchen. The radio sat on the table, minus the battery Yohan had stolen from it. Ryan knew they should have searched the Jeep for it. He hoped like hell Yohan had suffered before he died.

Wanting to fuck with them, scare them, make them sorry they'd fired him, he'd stranded them.

What they wanted was past the table. A door, identical to the closet door just outside the kitchen. A heavy-duty Master Lock barred their way.

Ryan wondered if any of the tools inside would be useful.

The Department of Lands manager Susan had talked to gave it a brief mention, a basement separated from the lodge's subfloor by a foot of concrete. It had served as an emergency fire shelter in the days the lodge had been a lookout post, but now it only served as storage.

Ryan knew the place had gone unused for years, and held a nagging fear that anything stored below would be rusted, aged to the point of uselessness. The lock was new, and that heartened him.

Ryan stepped back, drew up a foot, and kicked the door. The first kick echoed through the house and rattled the door in its frame. The lock bar hung a little looser. His second kick popped it open.

Weak light shining from the hallway lit the top of a staircase that led below.

A rip of cloth drew his attention away from the stairway, and he found Bill wrapping the kitchen window's torn curtain around the head of the poker. He lit it with a wooden match from a box of Blue Flames on the counter next to the stove, and started down, leading them into a vault Ryan hoped would turn out to be an arsenal, but thought would be little more than a gardener's toolshed.

It turned out to be a little of both.

⁂

The basement was small, Bill's torch lit it to all four corners.

Jim liked what he saw.

Hanging from one concrete wall was a trio of double-edged axes, all the handles painted green and stenciled with the letters WDOL. Two green handled machetes hung below the axes, one badly rusted, both blades chipped and dull. Bill grabbed one of the axes, holding it by the head like a cane.

A tool bench held drawers that turned out to hold nothing more useful than screws and nails of varying sizes, and a vise. A small can of lubricating oil sat next to a chainsaw. A brief moment of excitement ebbed as he saw the chain bar lying detached next to a metal file. The cutting chain hung like a grimy necklace from the open mouth of the vise.

The other wall was less promising, with a rusted hand saw, a claw hammer, a small pickaxe, and other less useful implements.

A gasoline powered weed whacker leaned against the bench, next to a push-broom and rake. Under the bench, a gas can and toolbox. The gas can was half full. The toolbox held a ratchet and an assortment of ratchet heads, a half-dozen screw drivers, adjustable and fixed size wrenches, and a small pipe wrench.

"Either of you know how to fix a chainsaw?" Jim asked.

Ryan shook his head.

"Camp could have," Bill said. "Not me."

"Hey, Bill," Ryan bent, picked up a small, grimy oil lamp. The half-inch of murky liquid that sloshed the sides when he set it on the bench promised a few minutes of light. Ryan removed the globe, turned the wick up, and Bill lit it with the makeshift torch.

The new, brighter light revealed the storage space under the stairs.

A stack of cardboard boxes stuffed with magazines. Jim pulled one out, blew the dust from it. A Playboy dating back to the late 1960s. He slid the boxes aside, and found a torch behind them.

An old weed-burning torch, connected by an old loop of hose to a small propane tank.

Yes!

Jim lifted the tank and was satisfied by the slosh of fuel inside.

"This'll do," he said.

Minutes later, the small tank in one hand, the torch in the other, Jim climbed the steps back into the kitchen. He had slipped the better of the two machetes beneath his loosened belt.

This is good, Bill thought, following Jim and Ryan through the lodge, the gas can in one hand, and the comforting weight of the axe in the other. Ryan carried an axe and the little pickaxe.

A couple of rifles, or maybe hand grenades and a bazooka, would have been better, but this was still good.

Bill liked their chances much better now.

They'd taken a hell of a chance, but it had paid off.

Kudos to Ryan.

In the main room, Jim fell back and let Ryan take the lead, his axe held before him, ready to use. Bill followed him outside, and Jim took the rear.

It was still raining, but not as heavily.

They walked single file to the stone fire ring.

The first step of Ryan's plan had gone better than expected. They'd found what they needed, and the gasoline was a definite bonus.

Time to get that fucker's attention.

Time to draw Rex out.

CHAPTER 20

Midnight Fight

The wood stacked next to the stone ring was wet, but Bill found enough dry wood in the stack next to the big cabin to start and maintain a good blaze. He piled them in a rough imitation of Ryan's kindling cabin of the night before, and splashed gasoline on the stack.

Then he lit the fire, hoping the flames would draw Rex out the way a porch light draws bugs. It did not.

They made a triangle around the fire, Bill facing the lodge and cabins, gripping his axe with both hands, Jim facing the mouth of The Devil's Tail, the torch wand in one hand and the machete in the other. Ryan looked out at the lake trail. The axe rested over his shoulder. The pickaxe leaned against the stump seat at his feet.

"Where is he?" Jim said, casting expectant glances from the trail to the canyon edge, and back again.

"He'll come," Ryan said.

Jim bent, opened the valve on the burner tank, then moved the head of the torch into the flames. The pilot light flared, blue and hissing.

They waited.

The rain stopped, the pattering drops went away. Sometime later the rain returned.

Rex did not come.

"We should check on Heather," Jim said.

Bill grunted his agreement. "Keep your eyes open," he said, and stalked away toward Casper's cabin.

With each step, Bill's sense of anxiety grew and took focus. They'd left her alone in there, for how long he wasn't sure. At least an hour. Maybe more. He had expected her to awaken in less time than that.

Maybe she'd woken up while they were in the basement and wandered off, or made a mad dash, thinking they were dead.

Maybe something worse had happened.

Keeping a sharp watch around him, Bill tapped the door lightly. If she were awake, she'd hear it. There was no reply to his knock.

Bill cracked the door open, stuck his head inside.

Heather lay on the bed, just as they'd left her. For a moment, he thought she had died. Her chest rose, then settled, and he realized what he had mistaken for death was nothing more than peaceful sleep. She'd quit tossing, quit muttering and crying out in her sleep.

Pleasant dreams, he thought, then backed out and closed the door.

"Sleeping," he said when he rejoined Jim and Ryan. "Let's let her rest."

Ryan set his axe down, stretched his arms and yawned. Bill was about to ask him what the fuck he was doing, when he picked up the smaller pickaxe and examined the pointed, half-moon head. He adjusted his grip high up on the handle, inches from the head, and gave it a test swing. Looked to Bill like he was practicing for a throw.

"When I was younger I could put a hatchet into a bulls-eye from fifty feet away." He smiled, a nostalgic little turn of the lips. "Won a few ribbons at the county fair. Impressed the commissioner's daughter so much she snuck out behind the carnie trailers and made out with me by the river."

"Was she any good?"

Ryan smiled, but did not reply.

"You still any good with that axe?" Jim asked.

Ryan took another swing with the pickaxe. "I could be if properly motivated."

"How about you, Jim?" Bill asked. "Any special combat skills?"

"Not unless you count laser-tag or paintball guns." He shifted nervously from foot to foot. "I don't suppose either of you have a smoke stashed away?"

"Sorry," Ryan said. "I thought you quit."

"I'm thinking real hard about starting up again."

"Camp might have an emergency pack in his glove-box," Bill said. "If you've got the balls to go get them, they're all yours."

Jim seemed to seriously consider this for a moment, then shook his head. "I'll wait."

"Weren't you in the Army, Bill?" Ryan asked. "If you're a Green Beret or something, now would be the time to tell me. It'd make me feel a whole lot better."

Bill scowled indignantly, but inwardly was pleased. His brief military experience wasn't something he put in his author's bio. Ryan had done his homework.

"I wasn't a fucking grunt," he said. "I was a Navy man."

It felt good that, despite the situation, they could still banter, still kid. It was better than drowning in the nervous silence.

"Besides, the only thing the Navy taught me was how to swab decks and get high off of industrial strength cleaners."

"God help us," Ryan said in mock horror. "He's a fucking Squid!"

Jim laughed, then stopped abruptly. "Guys?"

Bill and Ryan moved to Jim's position, flanking him, but Bill saw nothing.

"Jim, I don't…"

And there he was.

Standing at the edge of the woods, blending into the shadows. So huge that Bill had at first mistaken him for a tree trunk. Then he came toward them. Not running, but moving with startling speed just the same. His strides were huge, lumbering, purposeful.

Halfway to them, he stopped, turned, and looked at Casper's cabin.

"Fuck," Bill said, and started forward. "Hey, we're over here!"

Rex turned back to them, then to the cabin's door again, and started walking. Two giant steps brought him to the cabin's door. His right hand lifted the machete he'd used on Camp. His left reached for the door.

"*No!*" Jim stepped past Bill, stopping only when the hose at the end of the burner wand pulled tight. "We're over here, Rex. Come and get us!"

The giant froze at the sound of his name, his big green eyes finding Jim and locking onto him. Then he charged.

Jim backed away from the monster's advance, stopping when Bill caught him. Suddenly, Ryan's plan seemed the dumbest damn thing he'd ever been party to.

"Be ready," Bill said.

He moved a few feet to his left and advanced.

Ryan closed in on the right and shouted, "Hey handsome, I got your face!" He slapped the bear face mask hanging half out of his pocket, then raised the small pickaxe, gripping high up the handle.

If you can pin that fucker, Jim thought, *I'll take you out behind the lodge and make out with you.*

Rex's green-eyed gaze shifted to Ryan, and he changed course.

Jim raised the torch wand, finger sliding over the trigger while he waited for Rex to come into range.

"Hey, douchebag!" Bill shouted, drawing Rex's eyes to him. "You killed a friend of mine. Come on over big boy. Got some payback for you."

Rex stood, looking from one to the other.

Ryan moved first.

He leaned back, like a big league pitcher winding up for a scorching fastball, and let the pickaxe fly. It flipped handle over head. The flat of the pickaxe head smashed into Rex's face, splattering his nose. The blow rocked Rex backward, and when he opened his scarred and lip-less mouth in a silent howl, several blackened teeth fell out. He staggered, then moved for Ryan.

Bill lunged, sweeping his axe in an arc before him. His reach was short, the blow glancing, but the gash in Rex's side bloomed red.

The axe slipped from Bill's grasp as he stumbled, over-balanced, then fell.

"Fry him," Bill yelled, pushing himself backward through the dirt as Rex changed his course again, raising the machete in his fist.

Jim ran forward, dragging the tank behind him, and squeezed the trigger.

Nothing happened.

"Shit!" He released and squeezed the trigger again.

"Bill!" Ryan screamed. He raised his axe and stepped forward.

Rex's blade swung low as Bill pushed himself backward, and it bit flesh.

Bill screamed and rolled over. Digging his fingers into the dirt, he pulled himself forward. One of his legs remained behind.

Rex stood over him, drooling blood from his slash of a mouth, and raised his blade for the killing blow.

Jim slammed the burner wand against the ground. Dust puffed from its end, followed by the smallest of flames.

Plugged!

Ryan hit Rex from behind, the bit of his axe digging into his back. The blow knocked Rex to his knees, but didn't drop him.

Ryan lifted the axe for another swing, and Rex twisted, making a clumsy try for him. The blade whistled through the air. Ryan saw the swing and jumped back, and the blow that should have halved him tore the front of his shirt, drawing a long line of red across his stomach.

Jim dropped the burner wand and brought his machete down on Rex's head with all his strength.

It was like chopping a block of stone. The impact hurt Jim all the way to his shoulder. His blade split scalp, dug at the thick dome of Rex's skull, and bounced away.

Rex's free hand came forward in a long reaching arc that knocked Jim off his feet.

Rex stood again, a badly wounded animal, but still a strong one. He stood over Jim and brought his machete up, blade pointed down in a double fisted hold.

Yes, this had been a very bad idea.

Jim fumbled in the dirt for his dropped machete, and found the useless burner wand instead. The pilot was still lit. He pointed it upward at Rex, closed his eyes, and squeezed the trigger.

I'm dead! I'm fucking dead, Ryan thought, clutching at the tear in his stomach. Then he realized he wasn't. Another inch though, and he'd be holding his guts.

In another second it wouldn't matter.

Bill lay on the ground where he'd passed out while crawling to get away. A long, wet stripe of blood stretched from his severed leg to the stump where Rex had amputated it above the knee.

Jim was on his back, still stunned by the blow that had put him down. In a second Rex would gut him.

Then he'll take me, Ryan thought.

Then Heather.

The monster knew where she was, had sniffed her out like a predator sniffing out prey.

Ryan bent to retrieve his axe, and the flare of pain in his middle locked his muscles up.

The jet of flame to his left surprised him. For a moment his stunned brain refused to process it.

Jim's savage cry brought it into focus.

Rex fell backward, his face blistered red, scorched skin peeling away. His chest was burned down to muscle. The bear hide shawl hanging from his shoulders blazed. He beat at his face and shoulders with his massive hands while he backed away.

Then Rex turned and ran between the cabins, into the woods.

Ryan stood, stunned, while Jim scrambled on hands and knees over to Bill.

"Bill," Jim was careful not to touch Bill's cast-off leg, or the ragged stump to which it had once been attached. He grabbed Bill's shoulders and rolled him onto his back. "Ryan, help me get him inside."

Ryan moved. His first step was clumsy, unbalanced, the second step surer. By the third step he was sprinting.

The fight was over, but their night was not.

Rex lived.

They were stranded.

Bill was maimed, losing blood, and might not last the night.

Ryan and Jim each grabbed an arm, then carried Bill like a passed out drunk to Casper's cabin, leaving a slimy red trail in the dirt.

CHAPTER 21

Sweat, Blood, and Fear

Heather slept on, so Jim moved her quickly and gently as he could to the chair at the table while Ryan settled Bill back onto the bed.

"Give me your belt," Ryan said, pulling out a blade from his pocket knife.

Jim removed his belt while Ryan cut what remained of the leg of Bill's jeans away from the bleeding stump. He looped the belt and slid it over the stump. Ryan grabbed the loose end of the belt from his hand and cinched it tight.

Bill awoke from his faint, sitting up with a jerk, screaming.

"Hold still," Ryan said, "we have to stop the bleeding."

Bill looked uncertain for a moment, then his eyes strayed down to the source of his pain. He nodded, face set into a grimace, and lay back. He was sweating, biting his lips, his face bright red.

"We can't hold this tourniquet tight enough," Ryan

said. "We're going to have to cauterize it." He kept his eyes on Bill's eyes, unblinking. "You understand?"

Bill nodded, but said nothing. He continued biting his lips, and his cheeks were puffing out with his ragged breath.

"Jim," Ryan turned, lowered his voice. "Get the torch, and one of the machetes. You know what we have to do."

Jim did.

He went back outside, pushing back the fear that Rex might return by assuring himself that the sooner he had the torch and one of the blades in hand, the safer he would be.

He found Heather standing in the door, waiting for him, on his return.

She took the torch from his hand as he set the tank down. He wiped blood and sand from the blade on the leg of his pants, and held it out at arm's length.

He nodded to Heather. "Go ahead."

Heather pointed the torch wand at the sky and squeezed the handle, then turned the flame on the blade.

"He's going to be okay," she said.

"Yeah," Jim said, though he was far from certain.

"I can't hold it much longer," Ryan yelled from inside, his voice sounding strained.

"It's almost ready," Jim returned.

Come on, come on, Jim urged the heating steel.

The blood Jim had not managed to wipe clean burned away quickly, and within seconds the wooden handle grew hot. Jim fought the urge to drop it. By the time the top half of the broad blade started glowing a mellow red, the handle was almost too hot to keep hold of.

"That's good," Jim said, and Heather killed the flame.

They found Ryan and Bill waiting. Ryan was breaking out in sweat from the effort of holding the tourniquet, and Jim realized how much it must have hurt his torn stomach.

Bill's leg was propped on a doubled over pillow, the stump pointing toward the ceiling.

Jim dropped to his knees by the bed and brought the glowing blade forward, and hesitated.

Bill pushed himself up and glared at him. "Don't be a pussy, Jim. Fucking do it!" He pulled a fistful of his shirt up to his mouth and bit down on it.

Jim grabbed the machete's handle with his other hand, steadying it, and brought the hot steel to flesh.

Ryan kept his tight grip on the belt, but turned his head. He was close to the work, probably close enough to feel heat from the blade. The smell was almost pleasant, like roasting pork.

Bill clenched his eyes shut and screamed into his mouthful of cloth, but didn't faint again. He gripped the sheet underneath him and held fast.

When it was finished, Jim walked to the kitchen area and dropped the smoking blade into the sink.

"That should do," Ryan said, sounding sick. He loosened the belt, and let out a sigh of relief when there was no fresh blood from the cauterized wound.

Bill spit out his mouthful of cloth.

"I sure as ... sure as fuck hope so." He lay back down and closed his eyes again. "If any of you brought drugs with you, now would be a good time to fess up and share."

"Sorry," Ryan said. "The strongest thing I have here is aspirin."

"Casper had a bad back," Heather said. "He might have painkillers."

She scanned the cabin for Casper's luggage, found two bags at the foot of the bed, and searched them. "OxyContin," she said, and held up a small bottle.

Ryan took the bottle from her hand and opened it. He shook one out, frowned, and added another. He handed them to Bill, who chewed them with a grimace and swallowed.

Ryan went to the kitchen, opened a cupboard, and pulled out a first aid kit similar to the one in the lodge.

Jim walked to the open door for some fresh air, and Heather followed him.

"What happened?" she asked. "Did you fight … that man out there?"

"Yes."

"Is he…?"

"He's alive," Jim said. "But we hurt him."

"Do you think he'll come back?"

Jim considered that. If it were any other man in the world, it would have been a quick and definite no. But any other man would have been dead by now.

"I don't know," Jim said.

Yes, he thought. *But not yet. He'll be home now, licking his wounds.*

"We'll need more dressings," Ryan said.

Jim turned and saw Ryan smearing antiseptic cream on a sterile square of cloth from the first aid kit. He placed it over the charred stump, then unwrapped another. "I need more tape too."

Bill's eyes were still closed, but the strained look had

washed from his face. He looked relaxed, at rest. The OxyContin was doing its magic.

"I'll get it," Jim said. He hugged Heather, kissed her, and said, "Don't worry. I'll be back soon."

Jim picked up the torch, holding the wand in front of him as he walked toward the lodge.

Working out a plan in his head while he walked, and making a mental checklist of what he'd need to make it work.

To get them all the hell out of there before Rex came back.

"Take your shirt off," Heather said. She pulled clothes from Casper's bags, laying two clean white T-shirts on the foot of the bed, then picking up Ryan's knife. She wiped the blade clean on the bed sheet, and cut the white shirts into wide strips.

"I can wait," Ryan said, taking the first strip from Heather and wrapping Bill's bandaged stump.

Bill had drifted into a stoned sleep. Heather hoped it would last a while. When, *if*, they made it out of here, Bill would have a lot of pain to look forward to.

"No," Heather said. "You can't wait. I don't want that getting infected."

Ryan sighed and paused in his work to remove his shirt, gasping as the fabric pulled away from the clotting wound across his stomach.

Heather cleaned and bandaged the cut while Ryan continued wrapping strips from the white shirt around the stump. Then he wound a small roll of medical tape around the end of Bill's leg.

"That'll do," Ryan said, rising. "For now, anyway. We'll need to change them soon, unless we can get him to a hospital."

"Can we leave now?" Heather asked. "Is it safe?"

"I don't know," Ryan said. "Rex might come for us, or he might not. We have to try." He picked up Casper's bottle of OxyContin and examined it, reading the dosage, then giving it a shake to gauge the contents. It sounded full.

"It'll be slow. We'll have to make a litter for Bill."

"Can't we take Camp's car?" Heather asked. "At least as far as the road block?"

Ryan was silent for a moment, seeming to consider this. He walked to the open door and looked around outside. "I don't think so," he finally said. "Not with a flat tire. We'd bust an axle before we got far."

Heather was about to ask him why that mattered, any distance they made before that happened was a distance they wouldn't have to walk, dragging Bill along, but something else occurred to her.

"Then let's go get another tire from the Jeep first."

Ryan turned again to face her. "Even if we did that, we'd still have to walk most of the way."

Heather shook her head in frustration. "It's too far. Too *open*."

"I don't like it either," Ryan said. "We don't have any alternative."

"Sure we do." Jim walked in lugging three heavy bags, with a backpack strapped on behind. The torch wand's rubber hose ran into the partially unzipped top. He closed the door and set the bags down. Heather saw what looked like a rusted saw blade poking through the opened zipper. He turned off the torch's pilot light, then shrugged the backpack off.

"I went scavenging," Jim said. He bent and unzipped a filthy green canvas bag, revealing the motor of a small chainsaw. "If you can't put it together I'll use the handsaw, but either way we're clearing that road."

"What about the Jeep?" Ryan said. "You won't be able to push it all the way back here."

"I won't need to," Jim returned. "There's a wide spot in the road at the last turn before we wrecked. "I'll get it as far over as I can before I get another tire. That should give us enough room."

Ryan seemed satisfied. "Okay," he said, pulling the chainsaw and a detached saw bar from the green bag. "I'll see what I can do."

Jim shouldered the backpack again and picked up the burner wand, lighting the pilot with a Bic lighter. He pulled a crumpled pack of cigarettes from a front pocket and shook one out.

"Hope no one minds."

Jim smoked it down to the butt, blowing smoke out the cracked door, then flicked it outside.

"I'll be back soon," he said, and started out.

"Wait," Heather said, grabbing his arm. "I'm coming with you."

"Heather, no..."

"Don't," she said. "You can't work that thing," she pointed at the wand, "and push a car at the same time."

"I probably won't even need it," Jim said. "He's hurt. He might even by dead by now."

But Heather saw he didn't believe that.

"Good," she said, stepping past him out the door. "Then I won't need to worry. Let's go."

Jim shut the door and followed her away from the cabin grudgingly. The rain had quit, and in its wake left the mountain air chill, but clean.

"Wait," he said, and ran to the fire ring. An abandoned battleground littered with weapons, sprinkled with blood. Jim saw Bill's leg a few feet from the stone ring, lit by the mellow glow of the ebbing coals.

He found the small pickaxe close to where Ryan had dropped Rex's bear mask. He bent and snatched up the pickaxe, left the mask where it lay. Then he searched until he found the oil lamp, extinguished and sitting on one of the stumps that served as camp chairs.

Heather joined him.

"Take this." Jim handed Heather the wand and removed the backpack. "It's not too heavy." He helped her on with the backpack, tightened the straps to fit her smaller frame.

"Not much fuel left in either of these," he lifted the lamp and frowned at the diminished fuel level. "We need to conserve."

"Look," she turned her face to the sky. "The moon is almost gone."

A fragile amalgam of star and fire light glowed on her face, and Jim was struck anew with how lovely this woman was, a beauty his soon to be ex-wife could never match. It was something beneath the skin, something warm that radiated from her eyes.

Then she turned those eyes on Jim, and for a moment he forgot to breath.

"It'll be morning soon."

"Heather, I wish you would stay." He set the lamp down and took her free hand. "There is a chance he could come back, and if you fainted …"

His words drifted. He didn't want to finish that thought aloud.

"I don't want to lose you."

Heather smiled, a slight turn of her lips, and Jim couldn't stop himself. He bent down and kissed them.

"You're sweet," she said when they parted, "but you're talking like a macho asshole."

She turned her eyes back to the sky, then to the dark trail ahead.

The Devil's Tail looked like an open mouth, ready to swallow them.

"I won't faint," she said. "I won't let myself. And you can't keep me from going with you. I don't want to lose you either."

Ryan found the toolbox they saw in the lodge's basement in the second bag next to the first aid kit Casper had used on his broken nose. Without a clue as to what he was doing, Ryan tried to figure out how to fit the bar back onto the chainsaw. Last time he'd used one he'd been a teenager, and he'd never had to work on one.

"Hey."

Ryan turned, saw Bill sitting up on the bed again. He looked tired, but lucid.

"I can't give you more for a while," Ryan said, guessing Bill was about to ask for more OxyContin. "You're not going through all this alive just to overdose."

"I'm fine," Bill said. "That's some good shit. I can hardly feel my leg." His eyes turned to the elevated stump, and he laughed, a dry sound without much humor. "Where's Jim and Heather?"

"Clearing the road."

"What?" Bill said, almost shouted. The arms supporting him quivered, and he let himself fall back to the bed. "They should have waited until daylight. Fucking crazy. They won't see him coming."

"It'll be daylight in a few hours," Ryan said. "Be that long before we can leave anyway."

He found the bolts that held the chainsaw's bar shield on and started backing the first one out. "And I don't think Rex will come back right away. Jim burned him bad."

"If he's alive, he'll come back," Bill said.

"I know," Ryan said.

But please, not yet.

CHAPTER 22

The Small Hours

The way was dark, as before, but the pilot light from Heather's torch gave enough light for them to see the ground. The lamp hung dark, dead in his left hand. He wouldn't let himself use it until he'd found the Jeep. He'd need it then, first to push it out of the way, then to remove the last tire they'd need to make their escape.

Every now and then Heather would slow her pace and turn her face back to the sky, awaiting the dawn the way a child awaits Christmas morning.

Stars winked in and out of occasional breaks in the overhead boughs. Jim saw no noticeable change in the sky.

"Have you decided what you're going to do," Jim waited nervously for a reply, and when there was none, he elaborated. "You know, after we get out of here. Where will you go?"

"I don't know," she said. "But if he finds me again, I won't run."

Jim pulled the pack of cigarettes from his pocket and

lit one, trying to remember why he decided to quit. Not fear for his health, though the noticeable changes had been one hell of a perk.

Shelly. She had nagged him about that habit since they'd started dating, and he'd given it up in their final weeks together, not to mollify her, but to spite her.

"I don't want to run anymore," Heather said.

"You could come with me," Jim said. "You could come to New York, stay at my place if you want, or find a place."

"I've only been to New York once," she said. "It was a little scary. Too big. I had fun though." She fell into silence again, not accepting his invitation, but not declining it either.

Jim didn't push it.

"It's going to get out though, no matter what," she said. She sounded bitter, defeated. "I'll have to tell the police. Hope they believe me. Hope they'll stop him."

"Yeah," Jim agreed. If she didn't call the police, he would.

"The press will know within a week, and I won't have a moments peace." She took hold of his arm, startling him a little. "Are you sure you're willing to put up with all of that?"

Jim considered his words for a moment. "With the press hovering around you, he won't have much of a chance to bother you. And besides, when you're a mid-lister, any publicity is good publicity."

Heather laughed at that. Jim loved to hear her laugh. He knew he'd never get tired of that sound.

"Is that a yes then?"

"Let me think about it."

That was good enough for Jim.

Ryan figured out how to attach the bar to the chainsaw, and was putting the cover back over it before he realized he hadn't put the chain on it yet.

"Shit," he worked the first bolt back out and dropped it. It bounced off the floor, then rolled underneath Bill's bed. He reached under, feeling around in the dark under the bed frantically, almost in a panic that something hidden under there would grab it, pull him under. His fingers bumped it, searched again, and closed over it. He brought it out with a sigh of relief.

If this doesn't kill me, it will probably land me in the booby hatch.

Ryan suddenly realized how defenseless he was, sitting there unarmed while Bill slept his stoned sleep above him.

They'd left everything outside. The axes, the pickaxe, Rex's machete, dropped as he slapped the flames on his shoulders and face.

He remembered the machete Jim used to cauterize Bill's leg, and ran to the kitchenette. There it was. Stinking of cooked flesh, but a great comfort as he lifted it, the handle still warm, from the sink.

It lay next to him while he finished his work on the chainsaw.

Bill started snoring, distracting, but also a comfort for some reason.

He finished, almost positive he'd put it together right, and screwed the cover back on.

What next?

He was getting foggy, too little sleep, burnt out on adrenaline. Wanting a pot of hot coffee. Wanting his own comfortable bed in his own safe, psycho-free house even more.

What next?

The gas.

Ryan found the gas cap and unscrewed it. The tank reeked of gasoline, but was empty. The gas can was outside.

He set the chainsaw down like something fragile, something that might fall apart if handled too roughly, and took up the machete.

Knowing if he hesitated at the door, he might just freeze up, still be standing there, when Jim and Heather returned, he swung it open and rushed through.

The crisp air had an immediate, revitalizing effect, like a splash of cold water in the face. The sky seemed a shade lighter. Good. He pulled in a deep breath of that cool morning mountain air, and felt a little refreshed as he walked to the fire ring.

First, he gathered up the discarded axes, the pickaxe and machete were gone, presumably Jim and Heather had taken them. He hoped it was Jim and Heather that had taken them. Something else was missing, but he couldn't put his finger on what it was. The gas can sat where Bill had left it after lighting the campfire. He bundled the axes into the crook of his left arm, grabbed the gas can, and began his nervous trek back to the cabin.

Scanning the open area as he approached the cabin, seeing nothing alarming, just the open clearing, the canyon, a row of cabins, taken once more by abandonment, the lodge, taken by death. Camp's car, sitting at a slight angle on the remaining flat, the trunk still open.

Bill had mentioned a cooler stocked with Smirnoffs,

and he decided to make a second trip after depositing his haul. He took two bottles, twisting the top off of the first while he walked to the cabin again and drained half of it.

Then he remembered what was missing from their battleground.

Ryan's insides went cold, not the Smirnoffs he knew, not the mountain air. Fear, dropping into his stomach like a block of ice.

Rex's mask.

Ryan ran the last few steps to the cabin and slammed the door shut behind himself.

They found the wide spot in the road Jim hoped he hadn't imagined, and past the next turn in the road, Yohan's Jeep, mated to the fallen tree trunk, a grotesque sculpture in steel and wood.

Jim lit the oil lamp, feeling less vulnerable in the glow it threw around him and Heather.

"Hold this," he passed the lamp to Heather, and she lifted it over her head, increasing the comforting sphere of light.

Jim approached the driver's door and climbed in, groaning when he saw Susan's headless body lying on the hood, her legs still inside and dangling over the dashboard.

He felt a morbid urge to poke the leg, half expecting, in his exhaustion, to find a mannequin's leg beneath the jeans. Something hard, not the cold, doughy flesh of a corpse.

This isn't a movie set, he scolded himself. *Get your head out of your ass and do what you came to do.*

He turned the key, not expecting the engine to turn over. It didn't. He put the Jeep in neutral and climbed out again, rolling the window down before he closed the door. He took hold of the steering wheel, set his feet on the hard-packed earth, and pushed.

The Jeep would not budge, the grill was locked solid on the bark of the downed trees, impaled by a trio of stubby, twisted limbs.

"I'll help," Heather said.

"No, I'll get it." Not wanting her to see the piece of meat that had been a person laying on the hood. "When I get it moving, try to stay ahead of me. That's where I'll need the light."

Heather's eyes flicked to the Jeep's back window, and she nodded.

Jim readjusted his hold and stretched out with one leg, bracing his foot against the fallen tree, tensing, pushing.

A minute crack of wood, the scrape of the grille against bark, and the Jeep rolled free, slamming into the first jut of stone on the road behind them, and bouncing over it when Jim gave a second, wrenching push. The bounce set Susan's body sliding, and it hit the dust in a loose, flailing roll.

"Go, go," Jim shouted, and Heather led the rolling Jeep keeping to the center of the road.

Jim pushed, fighting the topography of The Devil's Tail, straining to turn and hold the wheel one handed as he met the turn in the road. It was tight, the front of the Jeep pushing him off the road, ducking limbs, tripping once and narrowly avoiding the tread of the front tire as he pulled himself up again.

The front bumper scraped stone, and they were on the straight again.

Progress was slow, and after five minutes of pushing, Jim collapsed to his knees, his arms quivering and calves cramping. The Jeep rolled on for a few feet, then stopped. Heather was there seconds later. She set the lamp on the Jeep's hood and bent down to him.

"Are you all right?"

He couldn't speak, so he nodded and held up one finger.

I'm fine ... one minute.

Heather dropped beside him, setting the burner wand aside, and pried his hands from his calf muscles. She massaged them, each in turn, until the knotted muscles loosened up.

"Much better," he said. "Thanks."

"We're almost there," Heather said. "It's just ahead."

"Let's move then," he said. The darkness seemed heavier the longer he sat.

Jim gave her a ten foot lead, and pushed again.

They came upon the place almost immediately. He saw the wide spot in the road, adjusted the wheel, and aimed for it. He didn't slow as the driver's side wheels left the road, though he again had to duck low limbs and stumbled on the rough ground. With only a few feet left to go, he gave the wheel a last tug, edging the front of the Jeep off the road, then pushed away, falling backward through the trees.

The sound as the Jeep came to sudden rest again the bordering trees was huge in the dead silence. He was on his feet again at once. The embrace of The Blues was cold, dark, and he knew what kind of monster those woods harbored. Pine needles were still drifting from the tops of the tree the Jeep had slammed, settling on the white paint of the Jeep's hood, the ground, and Heather's hair as she ran to meet him.

He brushed them from his hair. "I'm good. We're almost finished."

"Look, Jim." She pointed up.

He looked, and saw with a thrill of relief that the sky beyond the evergreen cover was brighter. Not much, but enough for him to see the difference.

If they could avoid the big ugly waiting for them somewhere out there, they would be on the way to safety by dawn.

Heather saw the small hint of relief on Jim's face, and felt her own small rise of hope. Despite what she had just seen. Or maybe just thought she had seen.

Something in the trees, just touched by the light when she turned at the sound of the crash and the shattering of the Jeep's back window as the back hatch bent inward.

A face, but not human. A bear's face.

When she'd looked again, bringing the burner wand up, it was gone. If it had ever been there at all.

But when she'd searched for Jim and not seen him, she'd been certain. The monster had come back, and had taken Jim.

It had not though.

So, Heather kept silent while Jim worked, digging

through the Jeep until he found the lug wrench and jack, then loosened the nuts holding the back tire.

She kept a close watch around them, watching the trees for another glimpse but not finding anything.

The mounting tension retreated a little as he finally pulled the tire loose and rolled it into the road.

"If I never have to spend another second in the woods again, I'll die a happy man," Jim said, and rolled the tire down the road back to the lodge.

"Ditto," she said, staying at his side.

Watching the road ahead of them, sneaking quick glances at the road behind.

Watching the trees.

CHAPTER 23

Cutthroat Business

Bill awakened for the second time, not sure where he was. Stoned, he knew that much. The Horrorfind convention?

No, he never got stoned or drunk at Horrorfind. Too much to do, Horrorfind was his show.

He wasn't wearing that damned florescent green t-shirt with *STAFF* written across it.

He was in a strange bed though, and it was god damned uncomfortable.

Bill sat up, feeling strangely unbalanced, almost tipping over on his side, and swung his leg over the side of the bed.

What the fuck?

He straightened the sheets that had bunched around his thigh, where another leg should have been. It was not hiding from him in those messed sheets.

The bear-man did that, he thought, and the other details piled around the image of the huge man with the machete.

Yohan pointing a gun in his face.

Ryan Stahl, Susan, H Casper, Heather Woods, sitting in a circle around a campfire, laughing at a story he and Camp told.

That was just last night.

Camp laying in two halves on the dirt floor of a hidden derelict cabin.

"Is it hurting you, Bill?" Ryan sat a few feet away at the table, nursing a bottle of Camp's Smirnoffs. A second bottle sat in the middle of the table, the label stripped off. It was filled with a clear, prismatic liquid, corked with a balled up strip of cloth, one end hanging down the side like a fuse.

"Hey," Ryan stood up, and as quickly as he could blink, Ryan was next to him, holding him by the shoulders. "No tipping over now."

"I'm fine," Bill said. He wasn't though. The OxyContin was kicking his ass.

Ryan guided him back onto the bed, and Bill let himself be led.

"Are they back yet?"

"No," Ryan said. "Soon … maybe."

"Maybe?"

Ryan returned to the table and tipped the bottle up, finishing it.

"Should be soon," he said again, and Bill watched as he picked up the gas can sitting under the table and filled the newly emptied bottle. "It's happy hour. Smirnoffs and cocktails."

"Did you top off the chainsaw yet?"

"Yeah. It even works." Ryan tore another strip from a shredded shirt laying on the table and shoved it down the bottle's neck. "I tried it while you were asleep."

"How long have I been out?" His voice was slurred, fading.

But Bill didn't catch the answer. Ryan's voice faded smoothly into a long past conversation he'd had with an editor. This had been before the first mass market deal, before the conventions, and fan letters, and Bill's well-earned reputation as the Madman of the genre, before the marriage that had calmed him down. The lunch meeting was the mid-point of a deal that eventually went south.

It's a numbers game, the voice of that editor, spoken around a mouthful of shrimp scampi, echoed in his head like something traveling through a long cavern.

Bill knew it was the truth, a hard truth that better writers than he was had been unable to cope with.

Right now the numbers were not good. They'd started with eight, nine if you counted Yohan, and were now four. Four to one, but this was not home turf. It was the Bearman's turf. Rex had the home-field advantage here.

Doesn't matter if you're a literary genius or a hack, if you don't rack up the numbers on your first novel, and quick, you're dead to this company. The editor, a white cloth napkin tucked into the front of his shirt and splattered with sauce and shrimp tail fragments, grinned his corpulent grin and drew a finger across his throat in a slashing gesture.

Cutthroat, he'd said, and laughed.

Drifting from the dream into an even darker sleep, Bill realized that he was just learning how cut-throat this business could be.

"How long have I been out?" Bill asked, and Ryan had to

take a moment to decipher his words. Bill was falling back into the OxyContin stupor again, slurring, mumbling.

"Not sure exactly," Ryan said. "A while."

Bill didn't reply, and when Ryan finished prepping his second Molotov cocktail, he looked around to find Bill passed out again.

For a brief, panicky moment he thought Bill had quit breathing, overdosed, or gone into shock. Then Bill spoke.

"Cutthroat."

Ryan shivered

A *tap-tap-tap* on the wall outside brought the shiver to a full skin crawl.

Not at the front door, or even the front wall, but the side wall, just beside the window, above Bill.

It came again. *Tap-tap-tap.*

Ryan did not go to the window, did not respond to the tapping. Just waited, a Molotov cocktail in one hand, digging one of the wooden matches out his pocket with the other.

Tap-tap-tap.

Someone lurking just outside, letting Ryan know he was back. But not coming in.

Why didn't he come in? It wasn't fear. They'd sliced him, chopped him, clubbed and burned him, and he still came back for them. If fear had motivated his flight from the fight earlier, it was short lived.

So why didn't Rex come in to finish them?

Thump!

Ryan jumped, but bit his lips to keep from crying out.

Rex didn't come in because he could not, and Ryan thought he knew why.

Ryan stayed put, ready to act if Jim and Heather came back before the monster left again.

Silent, because if he was right, silence meant safety.

Jim found himself looking ahead and planning his way around potholes and juts of rock that weren't in the oil lamp's sphere of light, and realized that morning had come while they walked, bringing shape and shadow back to the world. Soon he saw the opening into the clearing, a circle of lighter blue, like the mouth of a cave.

"Almost there," he said.

"Thank you," Heather whispered next to him, but not to him. It was the whisper of a woman kneeling before the crucified Christ, offering gratitude for an answered prayer.

Once as they ran down that final stretch, Jim, barely in control of the tire rolling just beyond his grasp, he heard a rustling in the woods to his right. When he looked, he found nothing but the trees.

The lighter shade of darkness before them widened, and Jim gave the tire a last, grunting push, sprinting behind it with Heather still close at his side. They followed it into the open air, and slowed as it wobbled, then tipped, spinning to rest as they stopped beside it. Jim stumbled, fell to his knees, huffing like a man just released from a stranglehold. Heather, not even breathing hard, set the lamp down beside him and put a hand on his shoulder.

"We made it," she said. "We're almost home."

"You're in good shape," Jim said. "You might have to carry me the rest of the way."

Heather laughed, then helped him to his feet.

"No stopping now. When we get back into town I'll carry you to our room."

Our room?

That was all the motivation Jim needed.

Crazy, he thought. *Half of my friends are dead and the man who did it is still out there waiting to get at the rest of us, and I'm suddenly horny.*

He laughed at himself, and when Heather gave him a probing look, said, "nothing."

People are strange. Writers are stranger.

Jim righted the tire and rolled it the remaining distance to Camp's Mustang, searched the open trunk and found the jack and tire iron next to the cooler.

"I'll start. Go tell Ryan and Bill to get ready." He thumped the tire with a fist. "As soon as I get this on, we roll."

Heather ran to the cabin, burning off the last of the adrenaline that had carried her off that damned road. She'd crash soon enough, she always did after high stress moments, but she was wired at the moment.

Wired and inspired. A hope junkie riding the best rocket of her life. She'd known trouble in her life. Five years of it with her bastard husband, but nothing this immediate or dire. Hope was all that had brought her through then, so she was not afraid to hope now.

She saw no light shining through the cabin's curtains,

but that meant nothing. They'd insulated the windows as well as they could against any light that might give them away to Rex. She tried the door, found it locked, and knocked lightly.

Nothing.

Knocked again, then placed her ear to the door, but there was no reply from within.

"Hello. Ryan, Bill?"

Quick footsteps from the other side of the door, then a click as the lock disengaged. The door swung out, and Heather stepped out of its way.

Ryan stood there, bloodshot eyes wide.

"Come in," he said, then grabbed her arm and pulled her inside. "Where's Jim?"

"Fixing the car," she said. "How's Bill doing?"

"In and out," Ryan said, and heather caught a whiff of alcohol on his breath. "Sleeping now."

Ryan went to the table and snatched up two bottles emptied of their original contents. Molotov cocktails, wreaking of gasoline as the liquid splashed inside and sloshed out around the wicks.

"Try and wake Bill. We can't leave Jim out there alone." He held the bottles between the knuckles of his left hand, letting them swing by his leg as he retrieved the machete from a pile of axes by the door. "Lock the door, and don't open it again until we tell you to."

Then he was out, shutting the door behind him.

Heather killed the pilot light on the torch wand, slid it into the open top of the backpack with the tank, and went to wake Bill.

Ryan ran in the morning glow. A sliver of fire lighting the trees on the eastern horizon signaled the coming of the sun. He ran toward the lodge, Camp's car. He heard Jim curse in frustration, the clang of metal against metal as he tried to work the jack.

He pushed himself a little harder, knowing if he could hear Jim, Rex probably could too.

Jim's fire may have blinded the monster, or mostly blinded him, he had been able to find his mask, but Ryan didn't believe it had taken his ears too.

Ryan passed the last cabin before the lodge, and saw Jim stooped beside the Mustang, cranking the jack's handle, lifting the flat tire, inch by inch, off the ground.

Rex stood mere feet away, at the edge of the woods, a great, still hulk. Only his head moved, turning side to side, not seeing, but hearing. Waiting for another sound to guide his steps.

Jim gave a final crank on the jack's handle and wiped his forehead.

The Mustang's frame groaned loudly enough for Ryan to hear as he closed in.

Rex's mask-shrouded head stopped, facing Jim. He raised his machete, not the twin of the one Ryan held, but bigger, rusted, bloody, and moved forward.

He considered the Molotov cocktails and dismissed them. Not enough time to light them, and Jim was in the way. He crouched and set them in the dirt next to the lodge, then ran for Jim just as Rex closed in.

"Jim! Watch out!"

The crank bar, not seated properly, slipped and gouged the side panel.

"Fuck!"

Jim shoved the crank bar back into the jack and twisted it, locking it on, then cranked. The car rose aggravatingly slow, and when the tire left the dirt, it gave an ominous groan. He'd forgotten to block the back tire, and expected it to roll back and fall. But it didn't. Camp had left it in gear, or set the emergency brake. It rolled an inch, then stopped.

"Jim! Watch out!"

He turned, startled, and found Ryan running toward him. Ryan wasn't watching Jim though, but something over his shoulder. Something behind him.

Still in his uncomfortable crouch, Jim jumped back and saw the blade of a machete slicing air where his head had been a second before, its handle completely swallowed by one of Rex's giant, meat hook hands. It glanced off the side panel, threw sparks from the jack's handle, and buried itself in the dirt.

Jim scrambled backward as Rex tugged the blade from the dirt, then felt Ryan's hands under his armpits, yanking him to his feet.

"Shhh." Whispered in his ear.

Rex followed them for a moment, then stopped, head turning side to side.

They backed away slowly, Jim watching in fascination as Rex's head turned like a radar dish on some sci-fi monster robot. Right, left, stop at center, right, and then left again. He moved forward, pointing his masked face toward the car and stepping around it, but he seemed not to see them.

Blind, Jim thought. *Or mostly blind.*

He saw the car well enough to avoid it, but didn't see them.

"Lead him away from the car," Jim whispered in Ryan's ear, and stepped aside.

Rex's head moved, facing Jim as his feet scraped the dirt.

"Hey, ugly," Ryan shouted.

Rex's face turned back toward Ryan, and he moved again.

Ryan backpedaled, and Rex stopped again.

"I'm over here, big guy." Ryan said.

Rex followed.

Jim waited while the gap stretched to ten feet, fifteen, and twenty, then moved back to the car.

He watched over his shoulder, marking Ryan and Rex's positions, while he spun the loosened nuts. Camp had taken good care of his Mustang, not a spec of rust slowed the nuts as he spun them off one at a time.

Looking over his shoulder, he saw Rex's silhouette standing against the darkness. Ryan was out of view, but Jim heard him coax Rex away with another taunt.

The old tire came off easily, and he slipped the new one on. He hand tightened the nuts, let the car settle, and used the tire iron.

Jim stood when he'd finished. The Mustang sat, salvation on four fully inflated tires.

It was the second most beautiful thing he'd ever seen.

The first waited for him back in the cabin.

Jim went to her.

CHAPTER 24

Quietly Now

Someone was shaking him awake, and just in time too. Still at that long ago lunch meeting with the editor, and someone at the next table was laughing. Bill realized he'd sat through the entire meeting in his underwear.

"Bill."

Fucking underwear dreams were the worst.

The editor seemed not to notice. He shoveled food, double fisted, into the open snout of his bear mask, into his mouth, all the time still talking.

There's a bumpy road ahead my friend, he said, and a mash of masticated food, broken teeth, and blood fell from his wide-open gob.

"C'mon, Bill. Get up!"

But he couldn't. The hands on his shoulders were small, smooth. A lady's hands, and her voice was soft, sexy.

Bill was already up, but standing was a different story. You couldn't conceal a hard-on under tighty-whities.

The editor slopped butter on a warm roll with a

machete. Blood from the rusted blade made a mystic swirl in the butter. Then the man shoved it thought the bear mask's mouth and made it gone.

The woman sitting behind him, who'd been laughing moments before, stood behind him now, shaking him. The restaurant facade thinned.

"You have to wake up, Bill. We're leaving!"

Her hands clenched and her fingernails bit in.

Bill opened his eyes, lying in bed, the stump of his terminated leg propped high, burning like it was on fire.

Heather released his shoulders.

"Jim should be finished with the car soon. Can you make it there?"

Bill sat up, and was able to accomplish the feat without a new wave of dizziness. The tradeoff was that a new lance of pain lit his stump, and a distant throbbing in the limb that was no longer there. "Can I borrow one of your legs?"

Heather smiled. "If it'll help, you can borrow both of them."

Ryan backed away, coaxing Rex along, and when the ground beneath him began to slope, he circled, around back to the flat.

This is where I let you off.

He walked in baby steps, watching Rex's silhouette, fade into the semidark. Standing, head turning.

Maybe I'll get lucky and the bastard will fall into the canyon. To that end he bent, plucked a palm sized stone from the earth, and threw it toward the abyss.

Rex moved toward the sound of the landing stone, out of Ryan's sight.

The line of fire on the east teased him, waved morning in his face, but was not ready to deliver yet. It was enough for him to make out the cabins though, and with a last glance back at Rex, he walked back.

He found Jim walking toward the cabin.

"Go get them," Jim said. "I'll wait at the car."

It would have been quicker just to drive to the cabin, but Ryan knew the sound would draw Rex back.

"Okay."

Jim stopped him. "Did you fix the chainsaw?"

"Yeah. I'll bring the handsaw too. Just in case."

Jim moved away then, and Ryan walked, scanning the clearing, back to Casper's cabin.

Heather heard the tapping at the front door she'd waited for, and rose to meet it. She found Ryan on the other side, sweating, near hyperventilating. A small tick twitched at the corner of one eye.

He put a finger to his lips. "Shhh." Then pulled her close and whispered into her ear. "He's out there, but he's blinded. If we're quiet he won't hear us."

Heather mouthed, *okay*, then went to Bill.

"Quietly now. He's out there but he can't see. If we can make it to the car without him hearing us, we'll make it out."

Bill took her hand and she helped him up, putting an arm around his waist to steady him. Ryan was there a moment later, taking Bill's other side. Together they lifted him, the tip of his shoe dragging the wood floor, and carried him outside.

A crescent of fire lit the eastern sky. Dawn had come and given the world a dusky life. They saw the giant wandering in the distance.

Jim waited for them at Camp's car. He did not look happy.

"Bill, do you know where the keys are?"

Jim saw the hopeful look in Heather's eyes falter and die.

"Fuck," Bill said, but without force. Remembering the situation. It was hard to forget with Rex standing in the distance.

The monster stood motionless now, facing the east. Still except for the barely perceptible motion of his turning head.

"Are they in your cabin?" Jim rephrased, trying to diffuse any panic before it surfaced. "I can find them if they're in the cabin."

"I don't know," Bill said. "If he had them on him down there ..."

"Then we'll have to go for them," Ryan finished.

"Wait," Heather said. She opened the Mustang's rear door, winced at the click the latch made, and helped Bill to the seat. She turned back to Jim, slipped the backpack off and handed it to him. "Just in case," she said, then hugged him. "Be careful."

"I will," Jim said. He shouldered the backpack and drew the wand from behind like a knight drawing a sheathed sword. He opened the pilot, lit it, and made his way, quietly as possible, to Bill and Camp's cabin.

Ryan watched Jim's form fade to silhouette against the rising sun and disappear into the second cabin from the lodge, then walked the short distance to retrieve the Molotov cocktails he'd left near the lodge.

Always keeping an eye on Rex.

Rex had not moved. He stood, facing he horizon as if hypnotized.

"Here you go," he handed the bottles to Bill, then pressed his machete's handle into Heather's hand.

The pickaxe lay in the dust next to the flat tire. He retrieved it.

Ryan considered their arsenal for a moment. They were all armed now, but even though he hoped to avoid another fight, if it came to that he preferred overkill.

"Sit tight, I'm going for the axes."

"I ain't going anywhere," Bill said. "I'll need more dope soon."

Ryan nodded. "I'll grab them too."

Watching Rex again as he walked back to Casper's cabin.

No movement. Stone still.

Ryan found the OxyContin bottle and pocketed it, then gathered the axes and handsaw into the crook of one arm. He lifted the chainsaw, he'd almost forgotten about that, he was so tired, with the other and rejoined Bill and Heather at the car.

Rex had not moved. Even his head was still now.

Could he see the sunrise?

An awful thought struck him, would the sunlight give Rex his vision back, or enough of it to find them again? If so they had mere minutes before he came again.

If Jim couldn't find those keys quickly …

As he crouched to set the chainsaw down the axes shifted in his arms, and one slipped from his hold, its head striking the chainsaw's cutting bar with a metallic *chink*.

The silence that followed was excruciating.

Heather stared over his shoulder, clapped a hand over her mouth, groaned.

Ryan turned.

Rex had turned toward them, facing them blindly, then took a step in their direction.

———

Jim searched Camp's bags again and again found no keys. Around the beds, under the beds, tore off the sheets and shook them. Nothing.

He turned the pockets out on a pair of pants next to the shower, and found a pen, but nothing more.

Giving up the search, Jim ran to the door, forgetting stealth in his panic.

———

He can't see us, Heather reminded herself.

But couldn't he?

Rex took another step in their direction, paused, and took another.

From the corner of her eye she saw Bill pass one of the

Molotov cocktails to Ryan, who dug a match from his pocket and readied himself.

The morning's glow was brighter now, direct sunlight moving slowly across the clearing toward them.

Rex's pace quickened.

He can't see us!

But Heather felt his eyes on her, and moved sideways away from Ryan to escape the weight of his gaze, real or imagined.

Rex stopped, and his head turned to mark her.

He can see us.

They'd blinded him, but not completely. He'd been lost in the dark, but the dark was gone.

There was nowhere left to run.

Heather lifted the machete and braced herself.

"Fuck me," Bill said, watching from behind Ryan as Rex came for them. "You guys get out of here." He considered the bottle in his hand grimly. "I can't get away, but I'll sure as fuck take that big bastard out with me."

"No," Ryan said. "I'm not leaving you here."

"Stupid son-of-a-bitch," Bill said, but was inwardly grateful. He didn't want to face death alone.

And death was coming for them, stalking them with the confidence of a practiced predator.

Then came Jim, bursting from the cabin ahead of Rex and stopping to face him. Sending a ball of fire toward Rex, not reaching the monster, but stopping him in his tracks.

"I couldn't find them!"

Damnit!

"Is there anywhere else he might have left them?" Ryan asked, his voice close to pure panic.

Then Bill remembered.

Camp had not slept in their cabin his last night. He had spent that night with Tracy.

"Tracy's cabin," Bill shouted. "He spent the night with Tracy!"

Tracy's cabin.

Heather heard this, and ran.

Not knowing where to start, not even *believing* she would find them. Their luck had been shit from the start, and she was giving up hope that it would turn around now.

She pulled the door open, marking Jim's position, only feet ahead of her now and holding Rex at bay with a burst of flame.

The keys were there, the first thing she saw as she stepping into the deserted cabin. They sat next to an empty coffee mug and foil condom wrapper. A half-dozen keys hanging from a monkey wrench fob.

"Yes!" She grabbed them and ran back outside. "I have them!"

"Good job," Jim said. He moved in front of her, and they backed away.

Rex paced them, kept out of reach only by the promise of more fiery pain.

"Can you drive a standard?" Ryan asked.

Heather nodded. "Yes."

Ryan had opened the driver's door, and she slipped in, ramming the key into the ignition and saying a little prayer as she turned it.

The Mustang roared to life, it's idle like a purring beast, ready to eat road and shit dust.

"Let's go," she shouted.

Ryan turned away from Rex and ran to the front passenger door, and before Rex could charge, a flaming missile hit the ground at his feet. Ryan's Molotov cocktail didn't shatter, but liquid flame gushed from its mouth, driving Rex back.

The rear door slammed.

"Ready," Ryan said, tittering manic laughter.

Jim laughed too, a sound of pure delight.

They'd done it. They'd survived, and they were getting away.

Heather gave her own primal *whoop* of triumph and hit the gas. Camp's machine responded admirably.

"Fuck you, handsome," Bill shouted as Heather whipped the Mustang around and put Rex behind them.

When Heather looked in the rear-view mirror though, Rex was gone.

CHAPTER 25

End of The Trail

It was still dusk on The Devil's Tail Road, but the Mustang's headlights cut an inviting swath of light through it. Heather guided them through at a comfortable pacc, not slow, but not dangerously fast. Bill braced himself as best he could, but the rutted road bounced him around the back seat.

Bill did not cry out, but Jim saw his face in the rearview mirror, gone scarlet with pain, and urged Ryan to give him another pill. By the time they reached the log blockade, he was fading in and out of consciousness again.

"Cover me, Jim," Ryan said, climbing from the safety of the Mustang into the vulnerable night.

Heather grasped the handle of her machete and opened her door, but Jim grabbed her wrist and held her back.

"Stay here. Be ready to drive, okay?"

Jim though she would argue, but she did not. "Watch yourself," she said, then kissed the side of his mouth.

"I will."

He followed Ryan and stopped beside him when he reached the spot beside the log where Susan's body lay.

"Start at that end," Jim said, giving Ryan a push away from Susan. "We have to hurry."

"Yeah," Ryan said, but didn't move until Jim gave him another gentle nudge. When he turned away, Jim bent and took Susan by the ankles, dragging her toward the trees. Out of sight, but not quite out of mind.

The chainsaw started, startling sleeping birds into flight, and Jim rejoined Ryan, standing behind him while he sawed. Watching the road behind them, watching the trees all around.

The scent of sawdust, pine Jim thought, was pleasant.

The splintering and groaning of strained wood drew his attention forward, and he saw that end of the tree settle to the dirt.

Jim stayed where he was as Ryan moved into the Mustang's headlights and began sawing the log down the center.

He kept his nervous watch, but saw nothing.

The high whine of the chainsaw settled to a rattling idle, and half of the blockade fell free to the hard-packed dirt. Ryan set the chainsaw aside and bent, rolling the short log to the side of the road.

"Just a few more minutes," Ryan said, and the chainsaw's high racket resumed.

Behind him, the Mustang's horn beeped, and Jim spun around, startled.

Heather pointed down the trail behind them, her eyes wide, wild.

A huge, lumbering figure approached, its outline crimson in the taillight's glow.

"Hurry, Ryan. He's coming!"

A heartening thump answered him, and the chainsaw's noise died away.

"Hold him off!" Ryan dropped to his knees and pushed the log, rolling it clumsily.

Jim raced to the back of the Mustang and gave a warning blast from the torch's wand.

The flames did not slow Rex this time, but drew him on.

"Okay," Ryan shouted, and Jim backed toward the car, taking the back seat next to Bill as Ryan took the front next to Heather.

Rex surged forward, grabbing at the Mustang, but catching their dust instead.

Heather watched the crimson-lit giant fade into dust and dusk in the rear-view mirror, then focused on the road ahead.

"We did it," she said.

"Yeah, we did," Ryan said.

"We're not out yet," Jim said from behind them. "Be careful. There may be more traps."

Heather saw the relief on Ryan's face turn to dismay, a mirror for her own frustration.

Hadn't they been through enough already? What next? What?

"We're almost there," Ryan said. "Can't be much farther."

Behind them, Jim said nothing.

"We're going to make it, Jim." She chanced a look from the road to the rearview mirror and caught his eyes with hers. "We're going to be okay. I'm going to find us suites in the best hotel in Lewiston. I'm going to fly Bill's wife here, and we're going to tell her personally what a hero he is."

She could see it all happening in that corner of her mind where stories are born, where they live, breathe, and become real. In her mind movie, there were no more roadblocks, no more fights for survival, no more death. It ended with a sure knowledge that wounded and beaten, Rex would become nothing more than prey for the greater beasts of The Blues. The cougars and bears and wolves would end his life and strip the meat from his bones.

The car parked sideways at the end of The Devil's Tail Road was not part of that reality, so she refused to believe it until Ryan tugged at her arm.

"Heather, they're not moving. Slow down!"

She did, feeling cheated at the delay in their great escape. When they were close enough to see the silhouette of a man in the cab, reclined in his seat and smoking what looked like the world's fattest cigar, she stopped and stomped the emergency brake to the floorboard.

"Wait," Jim said.

But Heather was not in a waiting mood. She wanted out, and this man, kicked back in the cab of his car as if he owned the mountain, was in her way.

Ryan seemed to be of the same mind. They jumped out in unison and approached the stranger's car. Heather clutching her machete, Ryan an axe.

"Move," Ryan shouted. "Get the fuck out of our way!"

The man seemed not to hear, or not to care.

"Damnit, move," Heather screamed. "Someone's coming for us!"

The stranger sat up, puffing his cigar, and regarded them through dusty windows. But he did not move. He opened his door and emerged, grinning.

No.

Heather refused to believe her eyes. They were lying to her.

"No!"

"You don't sound happy to see me, darlin," he said, and winked.

"What the hell is your problem?" Ryan shouted, advancing on him.

"Don't believe we've been introduced," the man said. "I am Dave Randal, Betty's *husband.*"

He shouted the last word, turning on Heather, making her flinch back.

"You probably know her by Heather Woods, but that ain't who she is. And you," he turned back to Ryan, extending his hand as if for a friendly shake, "are one dead sack of shit."

Heather saw the gun in Dave's fist then, and knew a handshake was not what he had in mind.

"Wait," Ryan shouted, holding up a warding hand.

Grinning again, Dave pulled the trigger.

The scene played out for Jim like a plot twist in a B movie. The psycho husband standing there, a smoldering cigar poking from the corner of his mouth and a smoking gun in his hand. Ryan's head exploding as the slug tossed him back like a rag doll, a grisly spray of bone and hair, blood and shredded brain splashing the Mustang's hood and windshield.

Heather, her machete still in hand, wilted to the dirt.

Jim, standing behind the open rear door, frozen, useless, until the next slug came at him, smashing glass out of the door window and punching a hole in him. Driving him to the dirt.

Jim hit the dirt screaming, the blood pouring from his torn arm like liquid pain.

"So, this is Betty's new life," Dave said. He came into view behind the open car door and laughed. "Making up fairytales and whoring."

He turned narrowed eyes toward Heather and frowned.

"She must be a decent fuck these days, because I read one of her books and she can't write for shit." He walked toward her, rolled her onto her back with a boot. "Figure she's been screwing her editor. Ain't that how your business works? Bend over and let your pervert editors give it to you up the ol' tailpipe?"

Jim moved while Dave's back was to him, rolled onto his stomach and dragged himself underneath the Mustang. He had no plan, only knew that when Dave faced him again there would be another bullet.

Dave continued, seeming none the wiser, but Jim held no hope of escape. He wouldn't be able to overcome him, and he would not run away and leave Heather and Bill behind. He would not do that.

"Got a little bit of bloodhound in me I think. I lucked

out at first. Saw her picture in one of those new shows, and she wasn't happy to be seen either, and I knew it was my Betty." He laughed. "Not the same picture she uses on the back of her books."

Jim rolled out from the other side of the Mustang, saw Ryan's axe lying next to where he'd landed, and crawled for it.

"You thought you could run from me again," he said, his voice low and cold, "but you left a nice little paper trail for me, and I followed it to Lewiston, Idaho. Asked a few questions, found your limo driver." He laughed again, as if recalling fond memories. "He didn't want to tell me anything, but I got it out of him. Yes I …"

Sudden silence, boots scuffing the dirt, the car door creaking as Dave pushed it shut.

A savage shout from the back seat as someone kicked the door back open, slamming Dave backward.

Bill.

From his place below the Mustang Jim saw Dave stumble, saw the gun tumble from his hand, and Jim moved. Suppressing a shout of pain, he rolled over his injured arm, out from underneath the car, and scurried for the dropped gun.

Not quickly enough.

The toe of Dave's boot caught him under the chin, bringing a flash of white that morphed not into unconsciousness, but only more pain. Something solid struck the back on his head, and when Jim's vision cleared, he was laying against the car, his head just inside the open door.

Bill was breathing heavily behind him. Under his breath, he said, "fuck."

Dave faced them, crouching, the gun in his hand again. "You see, it all works out in the end. It'll be like shooting a couple of gimpy fish in a barrel."

"Go on then, douchebag. Just shut up about it," Bill said.

Those words made the end just a little easier for Jim to accept. He relished the stung look on Dave's face, and braced himself for the end.

When the flash came, it was not what he'd expected. Momentary, blinding, then gone. Like sunlight glinting off steel.

Dave, screaming in all the surprise and pain that people like him never expect, but always feel in the end.

Something thumped to the dirt by Jim's feet.

The gun, its black metal now wet and red. Beside it, a hand.

Then Heather stepped in front of him, feet wide apart. An aggressive stance. The machete in her hand, its blade streaked with Dave's blood, angled for the next blow.

"Leave me alone you bastard!"

She thrust, and Dave stumbled toward the trees, the blade buried in his chest.

Before he could fall, two great hands reached from the woods and lifted him off the ground by his head.

Rex squeezed, and with a last squeal of pain, Dave's head popped like a lanced boil.

Rex tossed Dave aside and stepped from the trees.

CHAPTER 26

Misery Burning

Jim lunged for the gun, but Heather reached it first.

She brought it up, leveled it with both hands and fired. The slug punched into Rex's chest.

He stumbled back a step, slapped a hand over the wound, and moved forward again.

"No," Bill shouted, and tugged at Jim's shoulder. "Use this."

He slapped the wand into Jim's hand, the hose trailing past him to the backpack on the cab floor.

Screaming, Heather fired again, and again.

The bullets pushed at Rex, but did not drop him.

Jim fumbled the book of matches out of his pants pocket, struck with a shaking hand, and the pilot light popped to life.

"Heather, move!"

Heather dove to the side as Rex lunged again.

Jim squeezed the wand's trigger, and Rex burned.

He moved forward as Rex retreated, putting flame to every inch of the giant man. His tattered, filthy pants, the animal skin draped over his massive shoulders, the bear mask covering his ruined face.

As Rex fell back into the forest, the torch's flame weakened, then died. The fuel was spent.

Jim dropped the torch and joined Heather.

"Are you okay?"

Heather shook her head, and Jim followed her gaze back to Rex.

Impossibly, he was coming back. Still burning, but unstoppable.

"You persistent son-of-a-bitch." Bill stood outside the Mustang, leaning against it and balanced on his one leg. In his hand, the last Molotov cocktail. He threw it unlit, and it shattered against Rex's head, drenching him, turning him into a creature of flame.

Jim and Heather caught Bill as he lost his balance, then tipped. He threw an arm over each of their shoulders, and moving as quickly as his weight and their weariness allowed, they ran.

They didn't stop until exhaustion took their feet from under them.

The three survivors lay where they fell on the side of the primitive gravel road. They had run for maybe half an hour, maybe longer, and rested for only half as long, when Jim stood again to get a better look at the aftermath of their last fight. The fire had spread, and quickly.

How many acres gone already?

How many more acres between them and it?

If they didn't move quick, the fire *would* catch them.

Heather seemed to be of the same mind. She stood, brushing the dust off her hands, and reached for Bill's hand.

"My leg," Bill said, face bright red and sweating, "is killing me."

Your leg is probably burning up with the rest of the Hacks, Jim thought.

"Ryan had the painkillers," Heather said. "I'm sorry."

Jim took Bill's other hand. "We'll find a ride," he said. "Get you to a hospital and the best drugs money can buy."

They lifted him up, holding him around the waist while he looped his arms around their necks.

There was too much blood on the ground where he had lain. The bandage on the stump of his leg was sodden with it, leaving a striped trail of red as they moved again. If they didn't find a ride out, and soon, he would bleed out like a slaughtered pig.

Jim didn't believe they would find a ride out. Any ride they were likely to find out here would now be moving away from them, and the fire, as quickly as four wheels could carry them.

Fleeing the pillar of dark gray smoke rising into the sky.

Rex's funeral pyre.

Theirs too, likely as not.

Bill was passed out again, pain and blood loss this time instead of the blissful sleep of the drugged. They carried/dragged him onward, and found the first sign of human life a few miles down the road. A roadside campground, recently abandoned.

The sodden remains of a morning campfire, a stack of unburned wood, the remains of an aborted breakfast cooling on paper plates, on a bird shit spotted picnic table. Bacon, eggs, and a tin pot of coffee, left behind in their flight. The tent too was left behind, as if the owner expected the fire to reach them before he could tear it down and pack it.

Their dust still hung above the road before Jim, Heather, and Bill.

The comfortable early morning chill had become an oppressive heat. A dry, hot wind pushed against their backs. A wind that smelled of burnt wood, cooked meat, and fear.

Animals passed by, unseen but crashing through the underbrush of the forest.

Breathing had become a chore. An unkind wind pushed smoke above them, around them. Sweat stung Jim's eyes.

He could hear the flames now, still in the distance, but catching up, and Jim thought Rex would take them yet. Not the way he'd taken the others, but by default. By extension. His rage working through the flames, driving it onward like some apocalyptic beast.

Still chasing them.

Heather fell, and dragged Bill and Jim down with her.

Jim cried out as gravel bit at him, chewed through his outstretched hands, drank his blood.

But the shock of pain was a relief. The ache in his legs had numbed long ago, and his brain had as well. He'd been barely conscious, probably close to falling himself.

"Damnit," Heather said, but there was no heat in her voice, only exhaustion. Resentful, but resigned.

"Get up," Jim shouted. "We gotta keep moving."

"I can't," she said, but did anyway.

But she couldn't carry Bill another step, he knew that.

Jim took Bill's hand. It was cold, limp. He felt for a pulse, but didn't find one.

"Shit!"

Put the back of his hand under Bill's nostrils, and felt something, a small tickle of breath against his skin, or thought he did.

Maybe not dead, but as good as.

We should leave him, Jim thought coldly.

Instead he pulled Bill up by an arm and bent down, heaving him onto his back, holding his arm with his left hand, and hooking his right arm over the remaining leg.

They ran on, Heather pacing herself so Jim could catch up.

He knew it wasn't fast enough.

On they ran, and the fire rolled on behind them, closing the distance tirelessly. The flames knew no weariness, only the need to feed, grow, to move ever onward.

The heat was blistering Jim's back, and he saw steam

rising from Heather's blouse. Sweat boiling off into a salty cloud.

A new sound, challenging the crackle and roar of the fire, drew their eyes upward, and they saw the helicopter.

"Hey!"

"Down here!"

They screamed, Heather waving her arms above her head as they ran, but the men in the helicopter, gave no notice.

But it did not leave. It paced them, staying far enough ahead to avoid the inferno's heat wind.

"They see us," Jim shouted.

"I think so," Heather shouted back.

They see us, but they can't land.

But just when Jim decided he could run no more, the helicopter dropped.

"It's landing," Heather shouted. "Hurry!"

It dropped from view, but the next turn of the road revealed it again, setting down at a small clearing overlooking another canyon. A miniature of The Devil's Tail ridge. A moment after it landed, a man in a green uniform, Air National Guard, Jim realized, recognizing the military markings of the craft, jumped out and ran for them.

The guardsman met them at the road and relieved Jim of his burden.

"Let's go," he said, calm as could be, and led them, Bill slung over one shoulder, to their chariot.

An old bird, Jim thought, detached, as he helped

Heather up through the open cargo door, then followed her inside.

The guardsman knelt over Bill, examining him, checking for signs of life.

"We got 'em?" the pilot shouted from the cockpit.

The guardsman, their angel in green, nodded and twirled a finger over his head.

Let's go.

"Is he alive," Heather asked.

"Yes, ma'am. He's hanging on."

The helicopter rocked as it left the ground, heat turbulence buffeting them.

And as they gained air, Jim watched out the window, seeing the fire take the stretch of road they had traveled only minutes before. Higher up, he thought he saw The Devil's Tail Ridge in flames, a tongue of fire spitting orange death into the canyon below.

Let it burn, Jim thought as it fell into the distance behind them.

Let that bastard burn.

CHAPTER 27

Happily Ever After

Mr. Jim Eldridge

&

Ms. Heather Woods
Have the joy of requesting your presence at
Their marriage to be held on Saturday the 13th
Of April 2006 at two o'clock in the afternoon at
Saint Matthew's Cathedral in Cooperstown, New York
Services will be officiated by Pastor Dave Thomas
Followed by private reception and celebration

Jim and Heather

Jim and Heather married the following April, and honeymooned in Niagara, New York. There were plenty of tourists for them to blend in with, so they didn't attract attention. The scenery was beautiful, the falls gorgeous, their pace relaxed. This was as close to actual nature as either were likely to get again. Ever.

Bill Koch gave Heather away at the wedding, but missed the reception. He was overdue for a convention appearance in Baltimore.

Jim gave Bill the address of the hotel they had booked in Niagara, just in case he decided to visit.

Bill did not come, but on their fourth morning there, a package with his name on it did.

Jim and Heather,

Wish you could have made it to Horrorfind. You were missed. It was good to get back into things again, I've been cooped up too long. I understand why you passed though. No hard feelings.

My Monday night panel was standing room only, and they were lined up in the hallway outside to listen. It was tiring, reliving last summer for the entertainment of a roomful of drunk convention goers, but I needed to squash the crazy rumors that were cropping up. There were too many versions of our story out there. It was time to tell the real one. Maybe now that it's out there, the speculators will give it a rest. They'll forget all about it, eventually.

Until the book comes out anyway.

Did you hear about that? Some jackass wrote a novel based on what happened on Mount Misery. Hacks, he calls it. Heh!

Guy's got a surprise coming though. I'll be there at his first signing, and I am gonna put the largest prosthetic foot I have up his ass.

You two take care of each other, you hear? We will get together soon.

All the best,
  Bill

The letter came with a video, and after breakfast that morning, their last in Niagara before heading home to the city where both had deadlines looming, they watched it on their room's large screen.

Heather lay across Jim's lap, propped by pillows on the couch's overstuffed arm. Jim held her hand, caressing the fine lines of her palm, tracing the gold band on her ring finger with a fingertip.

She yawned once as they watched Bill on the screen, addressing the assembled crowd, telling their tale. Not his usual theatric style. He was serious, subdued.

To his surprise, Jim was wholly unmoved by Bill's telling. He had revisited every detail of the ordeal in countless dreams, and by comparison, Bill's telling was mechanical, bland.

Bill's audience seemed wholly enraptured though, as if his words had worked invisible hooks into them and bound them with strings he tugged at will.

The story was over in under an hour. The rest of the

tape was a collage of book signings, parties, and drunken Bill Koch rants. The final frame pictured Bill hobbling down an empty hallway toward his room, his green staff shirt exchanged for another with the words *Hail Satan* written across the front in bold, bloody letters. The camera panned in on the foot of his prosthetic leg. One of the many custom legs he'd collected, the foot was wide, red, the toes ending in long black claws.

Jim laughed.

Heather signed and shook her head. "He'll never change."

"No," Jim said, approving. "He never will."

Blue Mountain Blaze Contained –
Investigators Uncover Grisly Massacre.

Investigators from the Garfield County Sheriff's Office, Department of Lands, and the Washington State Patrol, acting on information gathered from three survivors rescued from last week's blaze, have located the wild fire's point of origin and determined the cause as man-made, but accidental.

Investigators also found several bodies, most yet to be identified, all murdered during a week long writer's retreat called The Hacks Club, at The Devil's Tail Lodge. Known to be among the dead are legendary writer H Casper, and local a man, Yohan Johnson.

The remains of long missing Sheriff Randy Frye were found as well, ending the twenty-year-old mystery of Sheriff Frye's disappearance. Yohan Johnson, a person of interest in the disappearance twenty years ago, is now believed to have murdered Randy Frye.

The survivors of The Hacks Club Massacre claim it was the Late Sheriff Frye's son, Rex, who murdered their companions.

Investigators are doubtful, however, insisting that the chances of Randy Frye's severely mentally handicapped son surviving twenty years in the wild is nonexistent, and that the atrocities were likely committed by Yohan Johnson when the vacationing authors found evidence of Mr. Johnson's past crime.

The search continues, but investigators have yet to find a body matching the survivor's descriptions of Rex Frye ...

Story continued on page 13

The End